"JUSTIN, WHAT IF JUST FOR TONIGHT WE DIDN'T HAVE to be married or divorced, or anything at all?" Morgan asked, her hands resting on his hips.

Then she slid her hands up to his chest. "If we didn't have to be Justin and Morgan, with all that history."

"So who did you want us to be?" he asked, grabbing her wrist and pressing her palm against his heart. "Scarlett and Rhett?"

"If you'd like," she answered.

He smiled. "So I could sweep you into my arms, carry you up a winding staircase and make mad, passionate love to you all night long? Is that the idea?"

A flush crept into her cheeks. That was *precisely* what she had in mind. "Why not?" she answered. "Tonight we won't be ourselves, just a man and a woman with no past, no future, only this brief moment of time together." She slid her hand from his grasp and grabbed his tie, pulling on it so he leaned closer.

"I'm offering you the chance of a lifetime, darling," she said softly. "A chance to flirt outrageously with your ex-wife without any repercussions. A chance to follow through on every mad impulse you feel for me without fear. A chance to fulfill your fantasies . . . and mine . . . with no strings attached. But you'd better act quickly."

She gave him a kiss on the chin. "You see, the offer's only good for tonight. . . ."

WHAT ARE *LOVESWEPT* ROMANCES?

They are stories of true romance and touching emotion. We believe those two very important ingredients are constants in our highly sensual and very believable stories in the LOVESWEPT line. Our goal is to give you, the reader, stories of consistently high quality that may sometimes make you laugh, sometimes make you cry, but are always fresh and creative and contain many delightful surprises within their pages.

Most romance fans read an enormous number of books. Those they truly love, they keep. Others may be traded with friends and soon forgotten. We hope that each LOVE-SWEPT romance will be a treasure—a "keeper." We will always try to publish

LOVE STORIES YOU'LL NEVER FORGET
BY AUTHORS YOU'LL ALWAYS REMEMBER

The Editors

Loveswept® 736

CAN'T FIGHT THE FEELING

FAYE HUGHES

BANTAM BOOKS
NEW YORK · TORONTO · LONDON · SYDNEY · AUCKLAND

With thanks to those who helped make this book possible: Laura Taylor, Patty Olney, and Deborah Wood, writers and friends extraordinaire; Lynn Peterson, the world's most understanding boss; and my agent, Rob Cohen, who never lost the faith.

CAN'T FIGHT THE FEELING
A Bantam Book / April 1995

If you would be interested in receiving protective vinyl covers for your Loveswept books, please write to this address for information:

Loveswept
Bantam Books
P.O. Box 985
Hicksville, NY 11802

ISBN 0-553-44488-3

Published simultaneously in the United States and Canada

PRINTED IN THE UNITED STATES OF AMERICA
OPM   0 9 8 7 6 5 4 3 2 1

ONE

He still wanted her.

Justin Stone stood in the doorway of his office and stared at the raven-haired woman sitting on top of his desk. With the telephone receiver pressed to one ear, head tilted back, short leather shirt hugging her tanned thighs, she had all the self-consciousness of a cat sunning itself in a warm spot. And he wanted her with an ache of longing that cut straight to his core, even though he knew such a desire was wrong. She belonged in his past, not in his present. And certainly not in his future.

They had both decided that a long time ago.

She crossed her legs, flashing an even wider expanse of thigh, and he smiled.

How long had it been since he'd seen her? he wondered, letting his gaze slide down the body he remembered so well. Five years? Six? It seemed like only the day before that he'd watched her wave good-bye through the window of the plane as it taxied down the runway in San José, Costa Rica. He hadn't been able to look at a white sandy beach or palm tree since without remembering the pain.

He took a deep, steadying breath. So . . . here she was again. His ex-wife, Morgan Tremayne. Sitting in his office in the American Literature Department at UC Santa Barbara, calling Lord knew who on his telephone. Probably some trendy boutique she'd discovered in Mozambique. Or a restaurant in Tangiers to ask if they'd deliver.

Hell, the whole world was her playground, while his was the dust of books and the dull tediousness of academia.

They had also decided *that* a long time ago.

He heard her laugh at something the other person said. It was a soft, tinkling sound, like crystal wind chimes clinking in the breeze. Then she turned and saw him.

Their gazes met and held.

"Let me call you back, Cookie," she said in that low, throaty southern drawl of hers that sent shivers down his spine. She dropped the receiver back in place and slid off the desk. "Justin. Long time no see."

He closed the door to his office behind him. "Hello, Morgan."

She was as beautiful as ever, he thought. A little older perhaps, but no less breathtaking.

She'd been a few months shy of twenty-three when they'd first met. He'd been a starving post-graduate student of twenty-seven who thought he'd discovered Byron's inspiration for his love poems in her shiny black hair and sky-blue eyes. It had taken him five minutes to fall in love with her and nearly six years to get over her.

He'd been working on his doctoral thesis on the works of E. J. Tremayne, a darling of the American literary scene who wrote with the cutting honesty of his fellow Mississippian William Faulkner and who lived with a passion that put Hemingway to shame. Tremayne had died too young, at fifty-six, on a safari in Africa, leaving behind three grieving ex-wives and a fifteen-year-old daughter. Morgan.

Eight years later Justin had been given permission by the family to study Tremayne's papers in his home in Woodville, Mississippi. That's where he'd met Morgan and fallen under her spell. She'd inherited her father's passion for living on the edge and enough money to keep her in pampered comfort for the rest of her life.

Loving her had been easy; keeping her next to impossible. It was like trying to hold on to water with your hands.

"I didn't know you were coming out to the West Coast," he said. And why should he? He hadn't heard a word from her since that day in Costa Rica.

"I didn't know myself until very recently."

She leaned up and gave him a kiss on his cheek. Her lips burned his skin. She still wore the same perfume, he discovered. Chanel No. 5. His hands itched to touch her.

Fighting the feeling, he maneuvered around her and headed to his desk. "So, what brings you by here?"

He straightened a stack of papers he'd been grading earlier for his freshman lit class.

She slowly walked around his room, gliding her fingertips over the back of an overstuffed armchair, then straightening a picture on the wall.

"Your office suits you, Justin. I like it."

He smiled again. The office was a cubbyhole filled to near overflowing with books and papers. Dust was at least an inch thick in some places, and he couldn't remember the last time he'd opened the curtains to let the sun shine through the tiny window in the corner. He even had a couple of dead plants on the credenza to prove it.

"It reminds me of Daddy's, all cluttered with books and stuff. Only there's no lingering scent of pipe smoke." She turned to face him. "You remember Daddy's office, don't you?"

He felt a wave of heat rise over him.

"It's where we made love for the first time."

Her voice was a husky whisper that set his

nerve endings on fire. Her fingertips skipped over the spines of some volumes of F. Scott Fitzgerald in his bookcase.

"Remember?" she asked.

Images flashed through his mind. The heat of a July afternoon in Mississippi. The coolness of the hardwood floor. The whoosh of a ceiling fan overhead, the silky smoothness of her skin below. Making love with her that afternoon had been wild and primitive and had felt so damned good. Its memory was carved into his soul forever.

"I remember," he said hoarsely, feeling an uncomfortable tightening of his trousers.

"Aunt Libby's still grieving over that Tiffany lamp," she added with a laugh. "Said it'd been passed down for two generations, and wasn't it a shame it got shattered to pieces and all."

She glanced at him. "You'd think she'd have gotten over it by now, wouldn't you?"

You'd think he'd have gotten over her by now, he thought.

He raked his fingers through his hair and frowned. "Morgan, why are you here?"

"Why, I wanted to see you, silly," she said, taking a step toward him.

A rap sounded on his office door, immediately followed by Sonia Garcia, his student assistant. "Excuse me, Professor Stone?"

"Yes, Sonia," he said, glad for any distraction at that point. He automatically straightened his tie and smoothed back his hair.

Sonia looked at Morgan, cocked an eyebrow, then glanced back at him. He didn't think he liked the knowing smile that slid across her face.

"If I'm interrupting," she said, "I can come back later."

"No, no. It's quite all right." He moved around the desk toward her. "What do you need?"

"The notes on the symposium. I didn't have time to stop by before my morning class. You'd asked me to retype them before delivering the packet to Dr. Capshaw."

"Of course," Justin said, motioning her back outside. "Let's see, where did I put them?"

He closed the door, leaving Morgan safely behind in his office.

The notes were sitting on Sonia's desk under a few pieces of his mail. She could have found them easily enough without his assistance if he'd only told her where to look, but he'd needed a few moments to clear his head.

He took a deep breath and closed his eyes.

Morgan was back.

By his estimation, for only five minutes or so.

But in that short period of time the old feelings had all come tumbling back. What did she want? he wondered.

And just how was he supposed to resist her this time?

❖————————❖

She'd almost forgotten how long his eyelashes were, how they'd flutter like butterfly wings whenever he lowered his gaze, making him the envy of every woman he met.

Smiling to herself, Morgan Tremayne hopped back on Justin's desk and crossed her legs.

She hadn't forgotten how broad his shoulders were, though. Or how they tapered down his hard, muscled torso to a slim waist. It took every ounce of self-control she possessed not to wind her arms around him.

Nor could she forget how warm his bare skin felt pressed against hers.

Or his lips, soft yet insistent, and how they could elicit the most amazing responses from her.

She clasped her hands around her knees and tried not to shiver.

The problem was, she'd always thought Justin Stone was too damned handsome to be a college professor with his sandy blond hair and too-green-to-be-believed eyes. He could be a matinee idol, maybe. Or some sex-symbol athlete racking up tons of money in toothpaste endorsements. But not a lit professor. Anything but that.

Her smile deepened. His female students must swoon whenever he entered the room.

She remembered the first day they'd met. How she'd thought the post-grad student from L.A. her aunt Libby told her about would be some bespectacled, gangly Don Knotts lookalike who'd bore her to tears with questions about her father's "genius." Instead, she'd found a blond, bronzed god who'd simply taken her breath away.

He still did.

She'd fallen hard. They both had. For the first ten months of marriage, they'd been deliriously happy. She wasn't sure what happened then. Justin had called it reality reasserting itself, though it seemed more like insanity to her. Whatever it was, things had changed.

He'd started talking about common goals and future plans and how hopelessly incompatible they were. She'd started telling him that the future would take care of itself, that it was the here and now he needed to worry about. They'd argued, of course—with the same passion they'd infused into everything else. Then, just as quickly as they'd gotten married, they'd flown to Costa Rica to get divorced. She'd honestly thought she'd never see him again.

And then her attorney had called . . .

She was going about this all wrong, she thought. She should have called first, eased him into it slowly. You can't just pop in out of the blue, say "hello, darling," and drop a bombshell that was likely to disrupt their lives forever. The situation called for finesse and timing. Tact.

She chewed her bottom lip. She couldn't begin to imagine how Justin would react to the news. With disbelief, certainly. That had been her first reaction. Then it had quickly been followed by the hope that maybe, just maybe, this would be their second chance to recapture what they'd once lost.

But what if Justin wasn't interested in second chances? Morgan thought, feeling a pang of uncertainty. What if he weren't interested period?

The door opened and he walked back in. His gaze slid immediately to her legs. He tugged on his tie and swallowed hard.

She smiled. Oh, yes. Justin Stone was still interested. No doubt about that at all.

"I hate to do this, Morgan," he said, averting his gaze. "But I've got a ton of papers to grade and—"

"How's Cappy?"

He glanced back at her. "You mean Leonard Capshaw?"

She nodded. "He was an old friend of Daddy's. He used to bounce me on his knee when I was in diapers and keep me in stitches with his recitations of Lewis Carroll's "Jabberwocky," especially the part about how it came whiffling through the tulgey wood. Cappy's eyes would get all wide, and he'd make the most hysterically funny noises deep in his throat."

Justin walked around the other side of his desk. "Dr. Capshaw's fine. I'll tell him you asked about him."

She slid around the desk to where he stood. "You never told Cappy about us, did you?" she asked softly.

He met her gaze. "There's not that much to

tell, Morgan. What happened between us was over a long time ago."

She reached out and stroked the side of his jacket. "But what if it weren't over?" She dropped her voice lower. "What if," she asked, weaving her finger through his buttonhole, "we were given a second chance?"

"But it is over." His voice was cold, almost angry. "Over and done with."

His hand snagged her wrist, and he pulled her off the desk.

"Look, I've got work to do, Morgan," he said, turning her toward the door. "Why don't you give me a call later in the day? Maybe we can get together for drinks or something before you leave Santa Barbara."

"Justin, wait."

She turned around. They were inches from each other, so close she could feel him take a sharp intake of breath as she brushed against him.

He released her arm and took a step backward.

"What is it?" he asked.

She stared at him for a moment, wondering what she was going to say. How she would phrase what possibly might be the most important words she'd ever utter in her entire life.

Slow down, she ordered herself. *Ease him into it.*

"Do you remember our honeymoon in New Orleans?"

She walked across the office to his bookcase and straightened several books of poetry that had come out of place. She slowly scanned the titles. Browning, both Robert and Elizabeth. Shelley. Lord Byron. She smiled as she reached the last. Justin used to murmur verses from Byron in her ear.

"What about it?" he asked.

"We were staying at this little bungalow in the French Quarter," she said. "We drank champagne, ate beignets and strawberries dipped in chocolate. And we must have made love for hours in that big canopied bed they had."

She shot him a glance. "You told me that what had happened between us was fate. Kismet. That trying to fight it would be like trying to ward off the wet of a hurricane with a toy umbrella. Do you remember?"

He stared back at her. "I remember," he said. "But I also remember what happened afterward. We got divorced, Morgan. A long, long time ago. Now, if you'll excuse me . . ."

He motioned toward the door.

"But that's what I've been trying to tell you, darling."

She slid the last volume of poetry into place and walked toward him.

"What is?" His forehead was drawn into a frown. "So far nothing you've said has made any sense at all. You show up here and start taking me on a stroll down memory lane. Do I remember this? Do I remember that? Why ask when we both know the answer? I'll carry your memory with me to my grave. So just what is it that you want from me, Morgan?"

"I'm not quite sure." Regret and longing colored her voice. "But for the last ten minutes I've been trying to tell you that we're not divorced. That we never have been. It seems the Costa Rican official who handled the paperwork made this tiny little mistake, and, well . . ."

She gave him a smile. "We're still married, Justin."

TWO

"We're what?"

Justin stared at her in disbelief, the color slowly draining from his handsome face.

"Still married," she said. "As in joint bank accounts and death do us part. As in—"

"How?"

The single word came out like a strangled cry.

"How could this have happened?" he asked. "I have a copy of the damned dissolution of marriage papers at home, Morgan. I know we're divorced!"

"I thought so too, darling," she murmured. "But I'm afraid we're not."

She placed her palm against his chest and gently pushed him back around the desk to his leather swivel chair. Another nudge, and he was seated.

She hopped on the desk, then gave her short brown leather skirt a good tug downward.

His gaze slid to her legs, then immediately away again.

She smiled. "I got a phone call from my attorney a couple of weeks ago with the news," she said, crossing her legs with a deliberate sensuality. "It all started when I had this tax audit."

He muttered a curse and tried to rise.

She pushed him back down. "Relax, darling, the IRS didn't find anything wrong with my tax returns. But I have a new accountant—her name's Elaine Brussard, and she's a real whiz with numbers—anyway, she found something odd with the dissolution of marriage documents I gave her, so she called my attorney, Boyd Paul Watkins."

"And?"

Justin's emerald-green eyes drilled into her. His hands gripped the armrests of his chair so tightly, his knuckles were turning white.

"And," she said, tucking a strand of her shoulder-length black hair behind her ear, "it turns out our divorce papers were never signed by the Costa Rican official who completed them. Boyd Paul did some checking and, well, it looks as though our request for a divorce was recorded as a request for a marriage license. Anyway, the point is . . ."

She reached over and brushed off some imaginary lint from his shoulder. She could feel the rock-hardness of his muscles through the lightweight tweed of his jacket. The clean masculine scent of his aftershave swirled around her. Her breath caught in her throat.

"The point is, we're still married," she said.

"Great. That's just great." He pushed her hand away and stood.

He walked around the desk and started pacing through the small office, from the window in the corner over to the oak bookcase against the opposite wall. Back and forth. Back and forth.

She slid around the desk and watched him. "Justin?"

No answer. He just paced across the office. Back and forth. Back and forth.

Then he muttered, "I might have known something like this would happen with you making the arrangements."

"Now, what is that supposed to mean?" she asked.

He glared at her but didn't stop pacing.

"It was your idea to get the divorce, Justin. Not mine. I merely suggested that if you were that eager to be rid of me, why didn't we fly to Costa Rica and have it over with in a few hours instead of letting it drag on for months."

"You know why this happened, don't you?"

He stopped in front of her and placed his hands on his hips.

She smiled. "Yes, but I have a feeling you're about to tell me anyway."

"You were flirting with the Costa Rican official who was supposed to be arranging our divorce."

"Flirting? Are you serious? I was only trying to be nice to the man."

"Nice? You straightened his tie and poured him coffee. You even called him 'dahling.' That's way beyond what I call being nice."

She grinned. "You were jealous!"

He stiffened. "Don't be ridiculous! I'm only stating the obvious. The man was following you around like some lovesick puppy. It's no wonder he screwed up everything."

"Are you actually suggesting that this is my fault?"

"Yes. No." He raked his fingers through his hair. "Hell, I don't know what I'm saying. I'm just a little upset right now, okay?"

She stared up at him. His jaw was clenched tightly, and a vein was beginning to throb at his left temple.

He *had* been jealous, she thought with amusement. Even nearly six years later, just thinking about the little bureaucrat in Costa Rica was enough to make Justin mad.

Wonderful.

"Darling, relax," she said, taking his right hand. "I spoke with Boyd Paul, and he's drawing up a new set of divorce papers. Considering what happened in Costa Rica and all, and the fact we've lived apart for nearly six years now, he thinks getting a divorce will be just a formality."

"Did he say how long it will take?"

She rubbed her thumb along the inside of his palm. He snatched his hand away as though she'd bit him.

"Ten days to draw up the papers," she told him. "Give or take a day or two. Once we sign them, it's practically official."

Frowning, he stared off at the bookcase. "The timing really stinks on this, you know."

She felt her heart stop. "Are . . . you . . . involved with someone?"

"Hmm?" He glanced down at her. "No, I mean I'm up for tenure with the university."

"How exciting!"

She grabbed his hand again and pulled him down beside her on the desk. Paper crackled as he flattened the stack of papers he'd been grading. Their shoulders brushed.

"That must be some kind of a record," she said. "A thirty-four-year-old associate professor being offered tenure after only five years."

He shrugged. "I worked my butt off, believe me. After the divorce, I finished my doctorate and got a position here at UC Santa Barbara. I needed something to get my mind off . . . things . . . so I threw myself into my writing, my teaching. I average four to five papers a year, serve as faculty adviser, steer a couple of committees. I really haven't had time to do much more than breathe since I got here."

She wagged her finger at him.

"All work and no play," she teased. "Don't you remember what that did to Jack?"

"Yeah, well, maybe I like being boring."

"Justin Stone, you are many things, but boring has never been one of them."

He looked at her for a moment, really looked, as though seeing her for the first time. Then he smiled that crooked smile of his that could send a woman into tachycardia.

"You've let your hair grow," he said.

His fingers stroked her cheek, then gently pulled a few strands of hair from behind her ear to let it swing free. His touch sent an electric shiver down her spine.

"It's nice."

His voice was laced with huskiness.

And his eyes, she noticed then, had deepened to a green so dark, they might have been black.

"Thanks," she murmured, leaning into him.

He turned away and folded his arms against his chest as though he were afraid of what they'd do if left unattended.

"So where are you staying?" he asked.

"The Biltmore."

"Nice place. I've had brunch there a few times. Have you been in the garden yet?"

She was watching his lips move, fascinated by the way they formed words.

"Ah, no," she said, feeling a flush climb into her cheeks. "I haven't."

"Make sure you do before you leave town."

He slid off the desk, then took her hand and helped her down.

"Look," he said, "I'll be tied up here for the remainder of the day. Do you want to meet me for dinner someplace?"

"I'd love to. Why don't I pick you up at your apartment around six?"

He hesitated a moment, as though his apartment were the last place he'd want her to be, then he relaxed.

"Sure, why not?"

"Wonderful." She met his gaze. "It's been great seeing you again, Justin."

She leaned up to kiss him. He turned his head at the last moment, and she got his cheek instead of his lips.

"Good-bye, Morgan."

He said it with such finality that she thought her heart would break.

She picked up her purse from the floor and left his office, gently shutting the door behind her. Seconds later, she rested her head against the cool plaster of the hallway wall.

Squeezing her eyes closed, she tried to drive the memory of his face, the scent of his cologne, his very presence itself, from her mind. She couldn't.

God help her, but she still loved him.

And she wanted him back.

When Morgan opened her eyes, Sonia, the student assistant who'd interrupted them earlier, was watching her curiously from where she stood next to a vending machine across the hall. Sonia was young, nineteen or so, with dark brown hair and eyes. She was sipping a can of diet soda.

"Hello," Morgan said. She walked over and held out her hand. "I'm Morgan Tremayne."

Sonia's face dissolved into a smile.

"The prof's ex. Yeah, I thought I recognized you."

Sonia took Morgan's hand and shook it. "I'm Sonia Garcia, his assistant."

"I thought Justin hadn't told anyone about us," Morgan murmured with surprise.

"He hasn't. But he keeps a picture of you two hidden in his desk. Doesn't think anybody knows about it, but we've all seen him looking at it."

"Really?"

So he does still care, Morgan thought, feeling her spirits soar. Or why else would he still keep their picture after all this time?

"Tell me, Sonia," Morgan said, slipping her hand into the crook of the younger woman's arm and leading her down the hallway. "About this picture he has of us, it doesn't have any dart holes on my side or anything, does it?"

Sonia laughed. "No. It's just a small snapshot. Like something you'd keep in your wallet. Real sentimental, you know?"

They stopped at the exit. Sonia eyed Morgan for a moment, taking a long swallow of soda.

"So, Morgan," she said, "you planning to rock his world again, or what?"

The memory of Justin's crooked smile flashed through Morgan's mind, quickly followed by the memory of his hands and lips touching every inch of her body. She felt a tingling warmth straight down to her toes.

Morgan gave Sonia a conspiratorial wink as she pushed open the outside door with a heavy creak of unoiled hinges.

"Oh, absolutely," she said.

At first Justin thought he'd been robbed.

Frozen in the doorway of his beachfront apartment, he cautiously glanced from the multicolored pillows tossed carelessly off the sofa onto the beige pile carpeting over to the rifled-through magazines on the oak-and-glass coffee table. Then his shoe bumped a mahogany-colored high heel. When he bent to retrieve it, he spied its twin next to the sofa.

And the brown leather miniskirt draped over his floor lamp.

And the silk blouse lying crumpled on the floor beyond that.

That's when he knew it was no burglar. It was something far worse.

He slammed the apartment door closed behind him.

"Morgan?" His voice was hard, angry.

They had created the game in the early days of their marriage as a way of making up after an argument. No matter how angry they may have been with each other, it had always worked.

Whichever one of them had gotten home first would promptly disrobe, then leave a trail of clothes for the other to follow. First would be shoes and shirts, then more intimate items of apparel like bras and Jockey shorts.

By then they'd be in the bedroom or the bath. Sometimes even in the swing on the back porch.

And more than in the mood to forget about whatever it was that they had disagreed about in the first place.

"Morgan?" he called out again. "I know you're in here."

He heard a door open.

"Justin? Is that you?"

Her lilting southern drawl was as soft as a caress, but he refused to let it get to him.

"Yes, it's me," he snapped.

Moments later she strolled into the living room, towel-drying her hair. She was wearing an old T-shirt of his that hung to her knees. It was loose and shapeless, yet damp enough in spots to cling to her tanned skin.

He couldn't help but notice the swell of her breasts, the curve of her hips. He drew a sharp intake of breath.

God, she was beautiful.

"Hello, darling," she murmured. "I didn't hear you come in."

She tossed the towel she'd been drying her hair with onto the back of the sofa and walked toward him.

"How did you get in here?" he demanded.

Tucking the high heel under his arm, he skirted both the coffee table and Morgan, then reached down and tossed the pillows back on the sofa.

"Your manager, Mr. Dukakis, let me in," she said. "He's such a charming little man, quite the storyteller too. And he thinks the world of you."

"Really?" he asked dryly. "Obviously he doesn't think that much of me, or he wouldn't be letting perfect strangers into my apartment."

He set the shoe on the coffee table, then straightened the stack of magazines, all too aware that she was standing right behind him. The scent of her perfume wafted around him, sending his senses reeling.

"But I'm not a stranger."

She touched his arm. Her fingers burned through his jacket, scorching the skin below.

"I'm your wife," she said.

"Ex-wife," he reminded her, prying her fingers loose. He grabbed the towel and tossed it at her.

"Ex-wife, Morgan."

"Wife," she repeated insistently. "At least for the next ten days or so."

He stared at her for a moment.

"Why are you here anyway?" he asked. "It's not six o'clock. And dressed like . . . that?" He waved at the T-shirt and damp hair. "Don't they have showers at the Biltmore?"

"Oh, Justin."

She sat down on the sofa with an exaggerated sigh. The towel crumpled to the floor at her feet.

"It was *such* a nightmare," she said. "They lost my reservations and had no more rooms available. They called around for what seemed like hours, but there's some convention in town. Shriners, I think. Or was it a group of podiatrists?" She waved her hand in the air.

"Anyway," she went on, "there's absolutely no vacancy to be found anywhere in Santa Barbara. I didn't know what to do, so I decided to come here."

She looked up at him through lowered eyelashes and gave him a smile. It was southern coquettishness at its best; even Scarlett O'Hara couldn't have done better wearing Tara's curtains.

But if there were no vacancies in the two dozen or so hotels and motels throughout Santa Barbara, he didn't know the difference between fiction and nonfiction.

And he had three degrees that said otherwise.

"You can't stay here," he told her firmly.

"Why?"

She reached for his hand and pulled him down on the sofa beside her.

"You have a guest room," she said. "And I don't have that much stuff."

"You have more luggage than the entire freshman class, but that's not the point."

"But I've already called Boyd Paul and told him he can reach me here."

"Then call him back."

"Justin, please," she said. "Ten days is all I'm asking you for. Until the divorce papers arrive. Then you can be rid of me forever."

Something told him that he'd never be rid of her. She'd already burrowed her way too deeply into his soul.

"Besides, darling," she said, smoothing the curve of her index finger down his cheek, "it would give us a chance to spend some time together. Talk things through. You once said our love was fated. Kismet."

She paused. "This could be our second chance for happiness, Justin," she said, and stroked his jaw.

"Maybe our last chance."

Her finger burned his skin. His throat felt parched. All he'd have to do was reach out and pull her to him. He knew she'd melt in his arms.

God, he wanted to rip that T-shirt off and caress every part of her body, wanted to make love to her right then and there.

But the price for doing that would likely be his soul.

"What makes you think it would work now?" he asked huskily. "Six years later?"

"Maybe because we're six years older, six years wiser."

She ran her fingertip over his lips.

"Maybe," she said, "because after having almost lost each other once, what we have will be more precious to us."

He captured her hand and pressed his lips against her palm. "Then again, maybe it would just destroy us completely."

He saw a shadow of pain cross her face.

He dropped her hand and stood to his feet.

"Look," he said, "I may regret this—in fact, I'm almost certain I'll regret this—but I guess it's okay for you to stay here until Boyd Paul sends over the divorce papers."

"Thank you, darling," Morgan said, rising.

She flashed him the kind of smile Scarlett always flashed Rhett when she thought she'd outsmarted him.

"And you won't regret it," she told him. "I promise. It will be—"

"Not so fast," he said, and walked around the sofa. "We need to establish some house rules first."

"Such as?"

He picked up the other high heel.

"Such as not leaving your stuff all over the

place," he said, retrieving her skirt from the lamp.

"But I thought you'd follow them like a trail of bread crumbs."

"And such as not using my closet as your own personal clothing boutique," he went on, ignoring her.

She grinned. "You mean your T-shirt?"

"And especially no waltzing around here half naked."

"You *do* mean your T-shirt."

She glanced down at the item in question, then placed her hands on her hips, causing the shirt to rise up her tanned thighs.

"And just what, may I ask, is wrong with the T-shirt? Why, it practically hangs down to my knees."

He felt as though his trousers were suddenly two sizes too small. "Trust me on this, Morgan," he said through clenched teeth. "The T-shirt has to go."

She laughed. "Well, if you feel that way, I'll just take it off." She reached for the bottom.

"No!"

"Okay, okay," she said, dropping the shirt. "Whatever you say."

She reached for the towel and draped it demurely across her shoulders, covering her breasts. Her blue eyes danced and sparkled.

"Now, are there any more rules I should

know about," she asked, "or does that about do it?"

"No long distance phone calls. International, I mean. Domestic's okay, I guess."

"No problem. I always use my credit card. Anything else?"

He thought about it for a moment. "I guess that's it."

"Fine. Then let me get dressed so you can take me to dinner."

"Dinner?"

"You did promise to take me out, remember?"

His gaze slid down her body again.

"Ah, sure," he said. "But I think I'll hit the gym downstairs for a workout first. You know, to work up an appetite."

Her gaze slid down his body. Slowly. And she smiled.

"Darling, I'd say it looks more like you need to work one off."

And then she turned and left the room.

THREE

They chose the Harbor Restaurant on Stearns Wharf, a Santa Barbara landmark that offered an unobstructed view of the marina and some of the best seafood in the state. It was a clear winter night with a million or so stars shining brightly in the sky over the Pacific Ocean, yet Morgan settled back in her chair next to the window and ignored the magnificent view.

She found greater pleasure in watching Justin's face as he read the menu.

"What looks good to you?" he asked.

You do, she thought with a smile. *With or without a garnish.*

"Hmm," she said, glancing back down at her menu. "I think I'll go with something light. Maybe the salmon or the sole in lemon butter. Which do you recommend?"

They discussed the relative merits of each until the waiter arrived a few moments later to take their order. Unable to decide, they settled on linguine with lobster sauce and a garden salad. After pouring them each a glass of Chablis, the waiter set the bottle of wine in its bucket of ice and quietly slipped away.

Morgan took a sip of wine, then set the glass back on the table. "You were really surprised to see me this morning, weren't you?"

He laughed. "Surprised doesn't begin to describe it."

The tip of his index finger traced a path around the rim of his wineglass.

"I'd begun to believe that I'd never see you again, Morgan. That the last memory I'd have of you would be at the airport in San José, of that plane as it taxied down the runway, taking you back to the States."

"I felt the same way."

She reached across and touched his fingers as they rested on the stem of his wineglass. The contact sent a thrill coursing through her.

"Although I never forgot you, Justin. *Never*."

He met her gaze. "And yet you never once called or wrote. In nearly six years."

She stared at him for a moment. "I was afraid," she said, withdrawing her hand. "Afraid of what you'd say."

Afraid he wouldn't want her back.

Or worse, that he simply didn't care anymore.

She was still afraid.

Oh, she knew he still desired her. But sexual attraction proved nothing. She wanted more than a brief affair with Justin. Much more. However, when she'd broached the possibility of a reconciliation to him back at his apartment, he had been, well, decidedly less than enthusiastic about the prospect. Which had hurt. Deeply.

In fact, the only thing that kept her going was the reminder that she had ten days in which to change his mind.

And she didn't intend to waste a moment of it.

"You? Afraid?" He smiled and took a sip of wine. "You're fearless, Morgan. Always have been. I'm talking the stuff of legends. A mighty Beowulf who girds herself for battle, then bravely faces a half dozen or so Grendels before breakfast. You see, I'm just the lowly poet who can only watch you in awe and spin tales of your exploits."

She cringed in mock horror. "Beowulf? I used to get Shelley and Lord Byron, now I get a lit major's worst nightmare."

He laughed again.

"But as long as you brought it up," she said, leaning back in her chair with her glass in her hand, "I've always thought of you as being more of a warrior than a poet. The strong and forceful type who goes after what he wants."

She sipped her Chablis and watched him over the rim of her glass. "Believe me, darling, Beowulf has nothing on you, the way you swept me into your arms and carried me off to your lair. I still get trembly all over just thinking about it."

A flush colored his cheeks. He took another swallow of wine.

"You know, maybe Beowulf's the wrong analogy," she said, sliding her glass back on the table. "You were more like some pirate in one of those historical romance novels. Bold. Brazen. Completely insatiable."

His gaze burned into her. She felt her heart flutter wildly against her chest.

"I guess that's because you brought out the pirate in me," he said huskily, and reached for her hand.

His fingertips began to caress her wrist. Liquid fire raced through her veins.

"Making me want to act out every fantasy I'd ever had."

"Hmm," she murmured, running the tip of a high heel along the hem of his trouser leg. "Maybe we could stop at a costume shop on the way home. I could be the feisty serving wench and you the lusty pirate home from the sea."

"Don't tempt me," he said with a growl.

"Pardon me," the waiter said, perhaps more loudly than was necessary. He slid a green salad in front of Justin. "You wanted French, I believe, sir."

He set another salad in front of Morgan. "Madame, the Italian."

Then he turned to Justin and lowered his

voice. "And may I suggest Sal's Costume Rental over on State? They're open till ten on weeknights."

Morgan giggled and released Justin's hand.

"Ah, thanks," Justin muttered, turning a peculiar shade of pink.

"My pleasure, sir." Stifling a grin, the waiter gave them both a little nod and left.

Justin glanced at her, and they both burst out laughing. Regaining their composure moments later, they settled back in their seats to eat. By an unspoken agreement the conversation shifted to lighter, safer topics: her family back in Mississippi; his parents down in Los Angeles; a movie they'd recently seen; a book they'd wanted to read but hadn't found the time to yet.

After the dishes were cleared and the coffee poured, Justin cradled his cup in both hands and leaned back in his chair. He watched her for a moment without speaking.

"So," he said, giving her a smile that warmed her to the center of her being. "What have you been doing with yourself the past six years?"

She took a sip of coffee. "Working mostly."

He shook his head. "My hearing must be going. It almost sounded like you said you had a job."

She grinned. "Very funny. I do have a job, and a damn fine one too. Remember that degree I had in child development?"

He nodded.

"I took a job about four years ago at a center for abused children in New Orleans. It's called For the Children. We have affiliates all over the country now, including one here in Santa Barbara. I hope to be able to drop by for a visit before I fly home."

She took a sip of coffee. "I work at the center three days a week. Sometimes more. It's so sad, Justin. Some of those kids will just about break your heart."

"You do counseling?" he asked.

She nodded. "And fund-raising. The center operates on a shoestring budget. I don't take a salary, of course—I doubt if the center could afford to pay me even if I'd let them. And I organize a couple of benefits each year to raise money. Convincing the haves to give just a little to the have-nots. I'm pretty good at it too. Which reminds me."

She propped her elbows on the table and rested her chin in her open palms.

"Would you care to make a small contribution to a worthy cause, Professor Stone?"

He took a swallow of coffee. "Perhaps you've confused me with some of your jet-setter friends," he said, placing his cup back in its saucer with a clink of china. "I'm just a lowly teacher with a lot of student loans to repay."

"You're a college professor about to receive tenure at a four-year university. And if I know you, those student loans are probably nearly paid off. So how much can I put your down for? Fifty? One hundred?"

He grinned. "I knew this was going to be an expensive visit."

"I take that to mean you'll contribute?"

"Be happy to," he said. "Remind me to write you a check when we get back home."

"Oh, don't worry about that," she teased. "Once I get a potential contributor in my sights, I never let him go without getting a signed check."

"Morgan Tremayne! By damn, it is you!"

Leonard Capshaw's voice boomed across the quiet restaurant with the explosiveness of a cannon blast.

Morgan turned in the direction of the sound. Leonard "Cappy" Capshaw, the widely respected head of the English Department at UC Santa Barbara, was hurrying toward them, his open trench coat flapping behind him like eggshell-colored wings, a big grin on his weathered, bearded face. He was a short, compactly built man in his early sixties, although she'd always thought of him as being at least seven feet tall, mostly because of his voice which had been known to rattle windows in their casings.

"Cappy," she cried with delight. She stood and threw her arms around him. "How long has it been?"

"Seems damn near an eternity, child," he

said, enveloping her in a gruff bear hug. "Damn near an eternity."

Morgan had known Cappy as far back as she could remember. He had met her father when they both worked for a short time at Tulane University in New Orleans in the early sixties. Her father had been lecturing on writing, Cappy taught lit. They'd struck up a friendship that lasted for years afterward.

Some of her earliest memories were stories of how they'd hunted together in the bayous throughout southern Louisiana, gone on fishing expeditions in the Gulf, and argued until the wee hours of the morning over what made one novel literature and another trash.

His hands grasping her shoulders, Cappy stood back to glare at her. "Why didn't you tell me you were in Santa Barbara?" he demanded.

"Well, Cappy," she said, straightening the collar of his battered trench coat. "I got here only today. Give a girl a break, why don't you?"

Justin, who had gotten to his feet when Cappy arrived, quietly cleared his throat. "Good evening, Leonard."

Cappy's hands slid off her shoulders as he turned. "Justin." His voice registered surprise. "I didn't know you knew Morgan, my boy."

Morgan's gaze shot toward Justin. *Well, I'll be damned*, she thought. He really hadn't told Cappy about them. Justin had kept quiet about their marriage for all these years, treating it like some dirty little secret.

Justin started to flush. "Well, we . . ." He was floundering for words. "You see, we . . ."

"Yes?" Cappy prompted. "Yes?"

Morgan let Justin stew for a little longer before she cut in.

"Cappy, Justin and I met when he was working on his doctoral thesis on Daddy, about seven years ago."

"Of course," Cappy said, smiling, though he still eyed Justin strangely. "I should have guessed. And a damn fine piece of work it was too."

He turned and asked the couple at the next table if he could take one of their chairs.

Justin met her gaze. His face looked pained, as though his lack of forthrightness had hurt him as much as it did her. "Morgan, I . . ."

"So, my dear," Cappy said, sliding his chair between them and resting his arms on the table. "Did Justin persuade you to participate in our symposium on American authors next week?"

Scowling, Justin sat down and reached for his water glass.

Morgan settled back in her chair. "What symposium is that, Cappy? Justin mentioned it only in passing."

Actually, his student assistant, Sonia Garcia, had been the one who had mentioned it, but why quibble over minor details?

"Well," Cappy said. "It's a week-long tribute

to twentieth-century American authors that Justin's spearheading. A revolving lecture series mainly, with discussions of not only the authors' craft but their lifestyle and contribution to popular culture. We're covering Fitzgerald, Faulkner, Steinbeck, and, of course, E.J."

Cappy nodded at Justin. "Justin's lecturing on that one. Even understand he has a few surprises in store for everyone too, though he won't say what."

"Oh?" She glanced at Justin.

He shrugged and looked away.

"I'm sure Justin would appreciate your participation, though," Cappy said. "Reviewing the program notes, offering little insights into your father. You'd be a godsend to him in terms of ensuring publicity, and I know you'd liven up that damn cocktail party on Friday night!"

Justin's head snapped back around. He stared at Cappy as though he'd lost his mind.

"I'm afraid that's completely out of the question," Justin said.

"What?" Cappy slowly turned.

"What I mean," Justin said, straightening his tie, "is that I'd love to have Morgan's participation in the symposium. But, unfortunately, she's going to be in town for only a few days on personal business."

He met her gaze. "Isn't that right, Morgan?"

She grinned. She just bet the sooner he had her on that plane headed home, the better he'd like it. But she knew a golden opportunity when she saw one.

Preparing for the symposium could easily take eight to ten hours a day. That was eight to ten hours a day that they'd have to spend together, working side by side. Coupled with the time they'd spend together at his apartment, that would give her nearly every waking moment for the next ten days.

Time enough, she hoped, to make him fall in love with her again.

Time enough to convince him to try for a reconciliation instead of re-signing the divorce papers.

"Don't be silly, Justin," she said. "I'd love to help. And I just adore cocktail parties."

"Excellent, excellent," Cappy said. He glanced around the restaurant. "Now, where the bloody hell is that waiter? I need a drink."

Justin looked as though he were going to choke.

"Order one for Justin too, Cappy," she said. "And you'd better make his a double."

Stifling a yawn at a quarter past seven the next morning—far too early for even civilized chickens to be awake, if you asked her—Morgan reached for the rose-colored terry-cloth bath sheet draped across the shower door. She wrapped the towel around her still-damp body and padded down the hallway to the kitchen in search of a cup of coffee.

What she found was Justin leaning into the refrigerator with his back to the doorway.

She smiled, forgetting all about how sleepy she still felt.

His hair was rumpled, flying in fifteen different directions at once, the way it always did in the mornings. He had on a pair of faded gray sweat pants that hung low on his hips. No shoes, though. And no shirt.

Only a hard, sculpted body that left her feeling weak in the knees and flushed all over.

She stared at him for a moment, watching the corded muscles ripple along the curve of his back as he moved, remembering how smooth and warm his bare skin felt beneath her fingertips.

Remembering other mornings a lifetime earlier, when they'd buried the alarm clock in the clothes hamper and unplugged the telephone so they could make slow, languid, uninterrupted love for a few hours more.

She felt the familiar surge of heat swamp her again.

She wondered if he still had the same erotic thoughts about her.

"Good morning, darling," she said huskily, taking a step toward him.

He jumped, banging his head against the refrigerator shelving. Muttering a curse, he slowly turned, holding a carton of eggs in one hand and rubbing his head with the other.

"Sorry," she said, grinning.

She took the eggs from him and set them on the counter.

"Did I startle you?" she asked.

"Ah, my fault," he said. "I guess I'd forgotten that you were . . ."

Then his gaze dropped, sliding from her face down to the curve of her breasts, which were just barely visible above the towel. He drew a sharp breath, held it for a moment, then slowly exhaled as his gaze dropped even lower, past her abdomen, past her hips and thighs, all the way down to where the towel ended just above her knees.

Her heart began to pound. She felt warmed to her core by his gaze.

It wouldn't take much, she thought. Just a casual slip of the towel. She knew he wouldn't push her away. Far from it. There was a fire burning in his gray-green eyes for her that was ten degrees hotter than the surface of the sun.

"I didn't forget about the dress code," she said, taking another step closer. "Really. I just got out of the shower and I wanted a cup of coffee. You know how I am in the mornings. A regular old sleepyhead."

She watched him swallow. "The coffee's in the pot," he muttered. "I, ah, think I'll go take my shower now."

Then he shouldered past her with a brush of

his bare arm against hers, sending a burst of fiery shivers cascading around her.

She took a deep breath. "I'm afraid I didn't save you much hot water," she said, glancing over her shoulder.

Moments later she heard the shower running and grinned. Something told her that at that moment he probably cared more about the cold water than the hot.

"Darling, stop scowling at me. This suit is downright dowdy."

Morgan was wrong on both counts, Justin thought.

First, the teal blue Chanel suit was not dowdy. A tad on the conservative side, perhaps, with its elbow-length sleeves, scoop neckline, and A-line skirt. But Morgan more than made up for that by spending the morning sitting on top of his desk, dangling her stockinged legs under his nose like a carrot on a stick. She couldn't have been more alluring wearing a black lace negligee and reclining against a big brass bed.

Which led him to his second point. He wasn't scowling. He was in pain from trying to keep his libido in check all morning. For the last hour or so, all he could think about was pulling her onto his lap and kissing her until she begged him to stop.

Something told him she was well aware of both facts too.

She was enjoying herself immensely at his expense.

"Did I say anything about the suit?" he grumbled, and tried to concentrate on his notes.

He couldn't do it, though. The words swirled around on the page, making them impossible to read. All he could see was the shadow of her high heel as she tapped her foot in the air.

"Not specifically, no. But last night you were having a conniption over the T-shirt, and this morning you were complaining about my wearing a towel when I got out of the shower. Although I really don't know what you expected me to do, Justin. Shower fully dressed?"

"What I expected is for you to obey my house rules the way you promised. That towel looked as if it would fall off if you took a deep breath."

She grinned at him. "Darling, I think you're letting your imagination run away with you."

Oh, there was no doubt about that.

He pushed himself away from the desk and stood. "Look, do you mind if we change the subject?"

"Fine. What do you want to talk about?"

"How about the damned symposium?"

He walked around the desk, putting a few more feet between them, hoping to cool the fire burning inside him.

"That is why you're here, isn't it? To help

me? Or was it to drive me insane? I keep forgetting."

She slid off the desk and moved closer. "Of course I'm here to help you. I've been thinking about the talk you want me to give, what I should say and all. I have an idea I'd like to discuss with you."

He tried not to look at her. He busied himself with straightening his notes on the lecture, which were scattered across the top of his desk.

"What is it?" he asked.

"Daddy always used to tell me stories when I was a kid."

Her voice was as smooth as velvet. It stroked him all over, fanning the flames.

"They were usually first drafts of his short stories and novellas. I was like his sounding board, you know?"

He glanced over at her.

"We'd sit on the porch in the evenings, watching the fireflies and swatting the mosquitoes. He'd be smoking that old pipe of his. And then he'd start talking. Daddy had the most amazing voice. He could do magic with it."

It was a characteristic passed on to his daughter, Justin thought, unable to tear his gaze away from her. Her voice was hypnotic. It left him spellbound.

"And his stories, oh, they were delightful."

She leaned against the desk, her shoulder

inches away from his. So close that the scent of her perfume nearly drove him mad.

"He made the characters seem so real," she said. "Like people you'd pass on the street every day or see in church on Sunday. I used to go into town and look for them." She glanced at him. "Does that seem silly?"

He swallowed hard and moved away, toward the bookcase this time. "No, I think it's wonderful. And it's a perfect topic for you to discuss. Showing E.J. as a father and not just this larger-than-life person."

"But Daddy was larger than life."

She followed him. She reached past him and smoothed her fingers along the spine of one of her father's books.

"I remember Mama telling me when I was about five that not all daddies brought home baby leopards for their children. It helped to put a lot of things in perspective, since I was beginning to wonder about the daddies of my friends."

"E.J. brought you a leopard?"

"Uh-huh. I named him Spot cause of, well, his spots. He scared the hell out of the catahoula hounds Daddy had for hunting. They kept baying and running around in circles, as if they'd treed the biggest bear in the world. The neighbors were just about as antsy. We had to donate Spot to the zoo in Jackson. I must have cried for a whole week."

He stared at her. At that moment he'd have

given everything he owned just to have been able to have dried those tears.

He forced his gaze away. "You should include the memory in your speech," he said. He walked back to the desk and restraightened the notes he'd tidied only moments before. "The audience will love it."

"Justin?"

Her fingers stroked his back. He shuddered.

"Thanks for letting me do this," she said softly, coming alongside him. "I know you weren't exactly thrilled last night when Cappy suggested I help you with the symposium, and I appreciate your giving in. You have no idea how much this means to me."

He stared into her face. He knew just how her skin would feel if he ran his thumb down her cheek. Soft and dewy-fresh. He began to ache from the want of her.

"Well, Leonard was right," he said slowly, his voice rough around the edges. "Including you in the symposium was a great idea. Still is. My only concern was whether we could work together or not."

"What do you mean?" She touched his arm.

He flinched as though she'd struck him.

"Why, Justin Stone, you're as nervous as a cat in a doghouse. Whatever is the matter with you?"

"You," he rasped out. His gaze bore into her. "Hell, ever since you got here you've been re-minding me of how good it felt to hold you, so that every time I get close to you, I just want to reach out and . . ."

He took a slow, ragged breath and closed his eyes. "Morgan, you've been making me feel things I haven't felt in years," he said, opening his eyes again. "I can't think about anything but touching you. Stroking you until you purr. I swear to God I don't know if I can control myself sometimes. I want to push you down on the floor and take you. Right here and now. Pound myself in you until there's no more me left. And no more you."

She stared up at him. A flush crept into her cheeks. Her lips parted. "So, who's stopping you?" she asked huskily.

He groaned and reached out for her. She slid into his arms. Their lips came together in a kiss that filled some empty spot deep within his soul. He forced his tongue in her mouth and probed its secrets. She tasted of the coffee they'd drunk earlier that morning. Sweet. Invigorating. He couldn't get enough of her.

His hands moved down the soft wool of her suit to the curve of her hips. He pulled her closer, wanting her to feel his arousal, wanting to grind her into him until she moaned with pleasure.

"Oh, Justin." She gasped. "I've missed you."

And he'd missed her.

He didn't know how much until that moment.

He pulled up her skirt, needing to feel her

bare skin, her soft, silky skin. His fingers glided up her thighs to the lacy garter holding her stockings in place. Dear God, what was she wearing? he wondered. His hands slipped over her rounded buttocks, feeling the silky fabric rustle beneath his fingers. He felt as if he were coming undone.

From a distance he heard what sounded like a rap on his office door. He ignored it, preferring instead to kiss her again. She rubbed herself against him like a cat demanding to be stroked. He pulled her closer, urging her hips against his. The knocking grew louder.

He groaned. *Go away*, he thought. Or maybe he said it out loud. He couldn't be sure. But moments later he heard Sonia Garcia's voice and that of another man, and Justin knew they had to stop.

He reluctantly pushed Morgan away as his office door swung open. Her skirt slid back into place.

Sonia's voice cut through the haze in his brain with the ease of a hot knife though melting butter.

"Adam Smiley, you're a real jerk! Can't you see they want to be alone?"

FOUR

Feeling as though her legs might buckle, Morgan leaned against the desk and stared at the slender red-haired man who'd just barged into Justin's office with an annoyed-looking Sonia hot on his trail.

"Adam, I'm warning you," Sonia said as she maneuvered in front of him. She placed her hands on her hips and scowled.

"If you don't leave right now, I swear I'll break something vital!"

"But I just need to talk with Justin for a moment," he said, trying to move past her.

"No!"

Adam glanced over her shoulder at Justin, who was straightening his tie and trying to regain his composure.

Adam came to an abrupt stop. He glanced at Morgan, who was smoothing the wrinkles out of her skirt. A flush crept up his neck to color his once-pale cheeks.

"Ah, hell," he said. "Did I interrupt something here?"

"What do you think, boy genius?" Sonia asked.

Morgan wanted to laugh, but she was having enough trouble just breathing.

She pressed her right hand against her chest and glanced at Justin, who seemed to be in much the same state of discomposure as she.

It was amazing, she thought, what one simple little kiss could do.

Although Justin's kisses were never "little" and their effect on her was hardly ever "simple."

In fact, the closest thing she could compare them with was when she'd taken a tumble out of an old pecan tree in her backyard at the age of eight. She'd hit the ground so hard, it had knocked the wind right out of her.

The only difference was she couldn't remember her heart pounding like a Sousa march or her skin tingling everywhere his lips had touched her.

Justin jerked his fingers through his hair and moved away from the desk.

"It's okay, Sonia," he said.

His voice sounded the way water did when poured over hot coals. Rough, with a definite sizzle.

"What did you need to see me about?" he asked.

Adam blinked a couple of times, his face turning an even deeper shade of crimson.

"Well, ah, I received a fax from the printers," he said. "They've incorporated the changes you requested to the program. To mention Miss Tremayne's participation, I mean."

Sonia shook her head.

"Jerk," she muttered a second time, then turned and left the office.

"They need immediate approval of the layout so they can proceed," he said. "It looks okay to me, but I didn't want to authorize it until you'd given your okay."

Justin nodded. "Where's the fax?"

Adam handed Justin several thin sheets of paper which Justin proceeded to review. Adam's gaze dropped to the floor.

"Look, I really do apologize for the intrusion," he said.

Justin shrugged. "Like I said before, it's okay."

Morgan felt a pang of conscience and gave Adam a warm smile.

"That's right," she murmured. "Why, Justin and I were . . . well, we were just going over our itinerary."

At least she hoped the kiss was an indication of the direction he wanted things to head between them.

She walked toward Adam and extended her hand. "I'm Morgan Tremayne. It's a pleasure meeting you, Adam. You're Cappy's assistant, aren't you?" she asked, taking a wild guess.

Adam nodded. "And the pleasure's all mine, Miss Tremayne."

"Morgan, please."

He positively beamed at her. "I can't tell you what a thrill it is to know you're participating in our symposium. E. J. Tremayne is one of my favorite authors. Why, I've read practically everything he ever wrote!"

"Oh, really?"

He nodded and then proceeded to prove his point by telling her about every E. J. Tremayne novel or short story ever published.

Still smiling, Morgan let her attention drift as the man prattled on.

She'd encountered plenty of Adam Smileys over the years, hard-core fans of her father's work who lavished E. J. Tremayne with the kind of adoration usually reserved for saints and old-time movie stars. She had learned a long time before that the easiest way of handling them was just to let them say whatever they felt compelled to say, cutting in occasionally with a nod or a smile.

She glanced at Justin, who had moved over to the bookcase. He was staring at the fax as though it were written in hieroglyphics.

Her smile deepened. Something told her that the kiss had made him take a tumble off the same tree limb she had. What she didn't know, however, was what Justin planned to do about it.

In other words, would he kiss her again, as she was hoping he would, or would he hightail it for safety the first chance he got?

". . . fascinated with the way he used setting as a secondary character," she heard Adam say. "Especially in some of his later works."

"Mm-hmm," she murmured, and walked over to stand next to Justin.

She felt him immediately tense. She reached for the fax, deliberately letting her fingers brush against his.

"How's it look?" she whispered.

He met her gaze, held it for a moment. She could see the desire still smoldering in the smoky depths of his green eyes.

". . . think 'Summer Heat' was one of my favorite short stories," Adam was saying, "although I always thought he should have gotten the Pulitzer for 'Amanda in Mourning.' What about you, Morgan? Which is your favorite?"

She ran her fingertips over the curve of Justin's wrist and felt him shudder. His eyes closed for a moment.

"My favorite story?" she asked, her voice growing huskier. "Hmm. That's hard to say. I always had a soft spot for 'Remembering the Bijou,' though."

It was one of her father's least appreciated stories and, to be truthful, it was far from being one of her favorites. She'd only said that it was because of its story line.

"Remembering the Bijou" was about a man in the throes of a midlife crisis who decides to wage an all-out battle to win the heart of his old girlfriend some twenty years after they'd split up. Most people thought it was about a man's desperate attempt to reclaim his lost youth.

But not Justin.

In his doctoral thesis he'd suggested that her father was trying to say that it was never too late to fight for love.

" 'Remembering the Bijou,' " Adam said. "Interesting choice. You know, I—"

Justin scowled and opened his eyes.

"Do you have the printer's telephone number?" he asked, walking back to the desk.

"Ah, yeah," Adam said. "Back in my office. Do you want me to call them and let them know it's okay to proceed?"

Justin shook his head. "I'll do it. Why don't I walk back with you and get the number? I'd like to run a few things by Leonard first before I call anyway."

Then Justin glanced at her. "It'll take only a minute or two," he said. "Half hour at the most. Why don't you start roughing out the talk you're going to give?"

Before she could so much as say "coward," Justin turned and left the office with a confused-looking Adam in tow.

Morgan sighed.

She should have known that Justin would try to hightail it to safety.

She walked around the desk to sit in his leather swivel chair. She reached forward and flipped on the switch to the computer. The internal disk drive began to whir as it went through its warm-up.

Then she smiled and leaned back in the chair with a scrunch of worn leather.

Not that running away would do Justin Stone any good at all, she thought.

To the contrary.

His resistance only made her want to try harder.

When Justin returned to his office forty-five minutes later, he found Morgan at his desk, working at his personal computer. She'd removed her jacket and was pounding away at the keyboard with a steely determination that brought back a whole slew of memories.

All of them pleasant.

He stood there for a moment and just watched her.

Morgan used to transcribe his thesis notes in the same way, as if she were out to set a new land-speed record or something. Of course, back then she had no choice but to type fast, thanks to his constant interruptions. Even though he'd known he shouldn't bother her, he hadn't been able to stop himself.

In those days all he could think about was touching her.

Kissing her.

Loving her.

He closed his eyes and took a slow, deep breath.

Things hadn't changed all that much either, he thought as the memory of their kiss flashed through his head.

Damn.

He squeezed his hands into fists. He shouldn't have lost control the way he had, he told himself angrily. He shouldn't have given in to the desire that had been building between them ever since he'd found her sitting on top of his desk less than twenty-four hours earlier. Hell, hadn't he learned his lesson the first time?

But he knew the answer to that one even before he asked the question. He hadn't learned his lesson. Not by a long shot.

And where Morgan Tremayne was concerned, he probably never would.

Truth was, he'd wanted her from the moment he had first laid eyes on her, all those years before back in Mississippi. They'd danced around each other for the better part of a month, though.

Flirting.

Teasing.

Lusting for each other.

When he'd finally kissed her that day in her father's office, it had unleashed something wild inside them both.

Something wild and passionate enough to shatter both her aunt Libby's antique lamp and his carefully thought out ten-year plan.

Nothing had been the same afterward.

Absolutely nothing.

All he knew—all he cared about knowing—was that he loved Morgan, that he couldn't possibly survive another day on this earth without her.

And for a few short months after they'd gotten married, loving her had been the closest thing to heaven he'd ever known.

Just as losing her had been a particularly gruesome version of hell.

"Hello, darling."

Her husky southern drawl sent a shiver sliding down his spine.

He opened his eyes to find her standing right in front of him.

Her sleeveless cream-colored silk shell gently hugged her body, curving around her breasts and showcasing those smooth, tanned arms of hers to near perfection.

Those long, thin arms of hers that could hold him like no one else ever could.

He swallowed hard.

"Where's Sonia?" he asked.

Morgan shrugged. "She said she had some errands to run."

He heard the dot-matrix printer begin to tap out a document transmitted from the computer.

She smiled and slowly ran her hands up his chest to rest on his shoulders. Her perfume swirled around him, making it hard to breathe.

His heart began to pound. The heat, the all-absorbing hunger, swamped him again.

"If you ask me," she said huskily, leaning closer, "she probably left so we could be alone. She'd seemed awfully upset when Adam burst in the way he did."

She kissed him on his chin. Her lips were as soft as butterfly wings.

"Come to think of it," she said, "it kind of annoyed me too."

He snagged her hands. "Look, Morgan," he said hoarsely, "I think we should talk."

He walked past her and headed toward the bookcase on the other side of his office.

"All right," she said. "But wouldn't you rather kiss me again?"

He glanced back at her.

She gave him that Scarlett O'Hara grin of hers.

The one that used to give Rhett fits.

"I know *I'd* prefer it if you kissed me again," she said.

And so would he.

Which, once he thought about it, was a large part of their current problem.

"I shouldn't have kissed you in the first place," he said, trying to stay on track. "It was way out of line."

Her blue eyes twinkling with mischief, she hopped up on the desk and crossed her legs.

"The timing may have been a little off," she said, "but the kiss wasn't. It was perfect."

"It was a mistake."

"According to whom? You certainly didn't hear me complaining about it, did you?"

"Morgan . . ."

"Darling, it was a wonderful kiss. Trust me. Maybe you're just concerned because you're out of practice. Come here."

She beckoned him closer.

"It shouldn't have happened," he said.

He stared at her for a moment.

"And it won't happen again."

She frowned at him. "Why?"

"You know why."

"But I don't," she said, her voice growing serious. "I really don't see why you're making this such a problem. I mean, we're both adults here. We're both free. And I know you still want me as much as I want you."

"Morgan, stop."

"Justin, you can't tell me that you didn't feel the same things I did," she said. "The same magic. The same passion. You can't stand there and tell me that if Adam hadn't barged in when he had that you and I wouldn't have made love. Because we both know better."

He averted his gaze. "But I don't want to feel those things," he said softly. "I don't want to want you as badly as I do. What happened between us was over a long time ago. We have to move on."

He turned back and met her gaze.

"Can't you understand that?" he asked.

She just stared at him. She was still smiling although the lights in her eyes had suddenly dimmed. The smile she was giving him now was strictly for show.

It was the kind of smile she'd perfected at those high-priced boarding schools her father had sent her to.

"It was just a kiss, Justin," she said quietly.

She slid off the desk and reached for the computer printout of her speech sitting in the black plastic tray beneath the printer.

"It was just one silly little kiss. Stop trying to make it sound like somebody should've called nine-one-one."

He stared at her for a moment longer.

"It wouldn't have helped even if I'd called nine-one-one," he muttered to himself.

He doubted if there were enough paramedics in the entire state to save them from themselves.

❦━━━━━━━━❦

Leonard Capshaw's weathered face creased into a frown. "The coffee's not that bad, is it?"

Morgan laughed and reached for her mug.

"Cappy, it's delicious," she said. "I'm just a little distracted tonight, that's all."

They were sitting on his redwood patio overlooking the Pacific Ocean, listening to the crash of the surf against the shoreline below and the distant laughter from a condo complex farther down the beach.

Morgan had hoped to spend the evening with Justin, but he had a committee meeting—a meeting she was certain he'd hastily put together just to avoid spending more time with her—and wouldn't be home until late. So she had accepted Cappy's invitation to dinner instead.

She couldn't stop thinking about Justin, though.

She couldn't stop thinking about their kiss, about how good it felt having his arms around her again.

Or about what he'd said to her afterward, that she was wasting her time hoping for a reconciliation.

She could still feel the dull ache deep inside her.

Cappy regarded her for a moment.

"How are the plans coming for the symposium?" he asked. "Are you enjoying yourself?"

"Oh, definitely," she said. "I drafted my speech this morning. I'll be talking about Daddy's personal life, my memories of him as a father. That sort of thing."

"Sounds fine. I'm sure the audience will love it."

"That's what Justin said."

She took a sip of coffee and set the mug back on the redwood table.

"And how about our professor Stone?" he asked, eyeing her speculatively. "Are you enjoying seeing him again?"

He took a sip of coffee. "I, ah, know how awkward it can be for some people to have to work with their ex-husband on a project," he added.

She stared at him in surprise for a moment, then smiled.

"Why, you sly old dog!" she said. "You knew all along, didn't you? And yet you didn't say a word last night in the restaurant. You sat there and let him stew, asking him how we knew each other and all."

He grinned. "I was hoping the boy would own up to it. Say 'She's my wife, Capshaw, and what's it to you any damn way?' But Justin's a private person. He prefers to keep the boundaries drawn between his personal and professional lives. I can respect that."

Cappy reached for his pipe. He tapped the bowl against the ashtray, added new tobacco from a leather pouch, and struck a match. The sweet aroma of burning tobacco swirled around her, transporting her straight back to her childhood.

She smiled.

"Your aunt Libby had written me all about him," Cappy said, "so I knew who he was when he applied at the university six years ago. It would've helped his career, Morgan, if word had gotten out that he was the former son-in-law of E. J. Tremayne, especially considering Justin's area of specialty. But he never said a word. Not to me. Not to anyone. Not even when I told him E.J. had been a friend of mine."

"Justin wouldn't," she said. "He never wanted to trade in on Daddy's name. He preferred to make his own way in life or not make it at all."

"Well, he has a strong sense of pride, I'll give him that. E.J. would have liked him, though. He's a fine man."

She smiled back. "I'd always thought so."

Cappy exhaled a stream of pipe smoke.

"So what happened between you two?" he asked. "If it's none of my damn business, just say so. But seeing how you were staring into each other's eyes last night made me wonder. Your aunt Libby told me she'd never seen any two people more in love than you and Justin had been. That it broke her heart when you split up."

She reached for her coffee mug and cradled it for a moment. Aunt Libby's heart wasn't the only one that had been broken.

"I don't know, Cappy," she said. "Maybe we

were too young. Maybe we rushed into marriage too fast."

She shrugged and sipped the coffee. "We had a lot of external pressures. Justin had to finish his thesis, and he was fanatical about not using my trust fund to pay our bills. And I guess I really wasn't cut out to be a little homemaker on a strict budget. I still wanted to go out every night with my friends the way I had in college, and Justin wanted to stay home and study."

Cappy smiled.

"I really hadn't found my niche yet, didn't know what I wanted to do with my life."

She set the coffee mug back on the table.

"Anyway," she said, "one thing led to another. We started to argue over the least little thing and, well, here we are."

She wasn't exactly sure why she'd decided not to tell Cappy that the divorce hadn't been legal, that she and Justin were still married. Maybe it was because she wanted to respect Justin's need to keep his private life private.

Then again, maybe it was because she was afraid that if she told Cappy about that, she'd have to tell him the rest.

That she was hoping the Costa Rican snafu would give her and Justin a second chance to make it work.

And by saying it out loud, she might jinx everything somehow.

"But you loved him," Cappy said softly.

"Oh, yeah."

She met his gaze and slowly smiled.

"I still do."

And she was going to get him back. No matter how many times Justin said differently.

FIVE

At seven-thirty the next morning, Justin turned into the kitchen and came to a dead stop.

"What's with the flannel PJs?" he asked. "You run out of towels and T-shirts or something?"

Morgan turned and grinned at him. "I'm just trying to obey your house rules, darling," she said.

Her velvety-smooth voice was as soft as a caress.

He tried to tell himself that it didn't get to him nearly as much as they both knew it did.

"What's the matter?" she asked. "Isn't it decent enough for you?"

She did a pirouette with her arms extended. The blue and white checked flannel pajamas were so big on her that the sleeves hung past her wrists and her considerable curves were all but nonexistent.

Yet he still thought she was the sexiest woman he'd ever seen.

"They'll do, I guess," he said, and smiled.

He leaned against the doorway, folding his arms against his bare chest.

"When did you get them?" he asked.

"Last night." She pressed the switch on the coffeemaker. "I wanted to surprise you with them but finally gave up around eleven."

She glanced back over her shoulder at him. "Tell me, Justin, do all of your committee meetings last until dawn?" she teased. "Or was this one special somehow?"

He shrugged. "We had a lot of ground to cover."

All of which had been neatly covered twice over by nine o'clock. He'd tried to make the meeting last longer, but his fellow faculty members had advised him—quite caustically too, he'd thought—that they all had lives even if he apparently didn't.

He'd driven around for a while, browsed in a late-night bookstore, then went for a long walk on the beach. Anything to kill time. Anything to avoid the inevitable. When he'd finally screwed up enough courage to come home, it was a quarter to twelve and Morgan had been asleep.

He'd tried to do the same thing that morning, namely avoid her, although he knew it was a losing battle.

He'd have to face her sooner or later.

Just as he'd have to admit to himself that what they once felt for each other was far from being finished.

"You know," she said, "there really was no need to hide out all night long. I promise I won't attack you again. Although you could give a girl a reason."

Her gaze slid down his bare chest to the gun-metal-gray sweat pants he was wearing. A wave of sensual heat washed over him.

"Or doesn't the dress code extend to you?" she asked pointedly.

"This is my house," he said, moving away from the doorway to stand next to the kitchen cabinets. "So the rules don't apply to me."

"Is that so?"

She leaned against the counter and smiled at him.

"Now, is that fair?" she asked. "I mean, you get to parade around here half naked while I—"

"I'm not half naked."

"The top half of you is . . . and I've got a pretty good memory about the bottom half."

He could say the same about her. The image was burned into his memory for all eternity.

Flannel pajamas or not, he knew just how her body looked unclothed. Firm. Tanned. With just the right number of curves. Her breasts were smooth and rounded. Not too large, not too small. Just the perfect size to fit in the palm of his hand. And her nipples would harden into little peaks when he stroked them.

He jerked open the cabinet and took out two mugs.

"But when I walk around here in a similar state of undress," she went on, "you get upset with me. Now, I ask you again, is that fair?"

He glanced at her. She was grinning at him, her blue eyes dancing. He caught a glimpse of her tanned skin through the opening of her pajama top.

God, he wanted her.

He wanted to pull her into his arms, wanted to weave his hands through her silky black hair and plunder her mouth as if he were some centuries-old pirate, just as they'd talked of his doing back in the restaurant. He wanted to make her moan his name as he caressed every luscious inch of her, wanted to make love to her with a frenzy that would leave them both weak-kneed and sated.

He tightened his grip on the coffee mugs.

"Life's not fair, Morgan," he said. "If it were, our divorce would've gone through without a problem."

And he wouldn't be standing there some six years later, wanting her so bad that it hurt.

She frowned at him. "You make it sound as if I planned it that way. I was just as surprised as you were when Boyd Paul broke the news to me."

The coffee had begun to drip into the glass pot. The aroma quickly filled the small kitchen.

"Now give me the mugs, darling," she said, "before you shatter them or something."

Her fingers lightly brushed against his hands as she took the ceramic mugs from him, yet his body responded with an immediate arousal. He took a slow, deep breath.

"Oh, before I forget," she said. "I'll need your check this morning."

She'd turned back to the coffeemaker. Her voice sounded so damn normal, he thought with amazement. As if she weren't the least bit affected by him.

As if the desire coursing through his veins right now weren't coursing through her own.

"What check?" he asked hoarsely.

"The one you promised me for my organization, For the Children. Now, Justin Stone, don't you dare say that you don't remember promising me two hundred dollars."

"It was fifty, and I didn't forget."

She glanced back at him and smiled.

"I'll write the check this morning," he said.

"Good. I promised Cookie—she's our operations manager—that I'd overnight it to her along with some other papers I need to pick up from our Santa Barbara affiliate. You know," she said, thinking out loud, "I should have probably hit Cappy up for a donation last night."

He frowned. "I thought you went shopping last night."

"Hmm? Oh, I did. But that was earlier, before my date with Cappy."

He stared at her for a moment, feeling an icy cold settle in the pit of his stomach.

"For crissakes, Morgan," he said, "the man's old enough to be your father!"

She stared back at him as if she thought he'd completely lost his mind.

Which he probably had.

"Darling, whatever are you growling about?" she asked. "I didn't mean that Cappy and I had a 'date' date. We only had a dinner date. To talk over old times."

She regarded him again for a few seconds, then smiled. "Believe me," she said. "There's no reason for you to be jealous of him. None whatsoever."

"I'm not jealous."

"Oh?" She grinned and handed him a mug of coffee. "Then why did you suddenly look as though you wanted to pummel the chair of the English Department into a bloody pulp?"

She picked up her own mug and walked out of the kitchen.

"I didn't . . . want to pummel him," he said. "Maybe just slap him around a bit."

Because she was right. He *was* jealous. Positively green with it at the thought of Morgan going out with Leonard Capshaw, or any other man, for that matter.

He raked his fingers through his hair.

Damn.

Maybe he should forget the coffee and take another cold shower.

Morgan attached the top of her stockings to her lace garter and stood, slipping her feet into her gray pumps. She smoothed out the wrinkles in her silk teddy, then reached for the smoke-colored wool sweater-dress lying across the bed.

A knock sounded on the bedroom door.

She glanced over her shoulder in time to see the door open and Justin stick his head into the room.

"Morgan, here's the check I promised . . ."

His voice faded away. He came to a complete stop. And stared at her.

She slowly turned to face him.

She could have reached for the pajama top lying on the bed. Just as easily as he could have left the room.

But they did neither.

His gaze slowly slid down her body, scorching through the flimsy silk-and-lace teddy to her bare skin. Caressing her. Making her burn from a look that was so intimate, she wanted to shudder.

She heard him draw in his breath sharply.

"Damn," he muttered.

Then she smiled.

His eyes had darkened to a gray-green; his body turned rigid with tension. She could see the unmistakable hardness of his arousal through his sweat pants. She knew he wanted her.

Wanted her as badly as she did him.

What she didn't know was if he was ready to admit it yet.

She took a step toward him.

"I . . . ah . . . here," he said.

He put the check on the dresser, where it fluttered to the floor. Then he turned and left the bedroom, closing the door firmly behind him.

And a few seconds later she heard the sound of the shower running.

She grinned and picked up the check from the floor.

Poor baby, she thought.

If this went on much longer, his water bill would likely rival the national debt.

Several hours later Morgan quietly slipped into an empty seat at the back of the auditorium just as Justin's Introduction to American Literature class was winding down.

She would have preferred to sit up front and listen to the whole thing, but she hadn't been given the luxury. When she'd told him she wanted to attend his morning lecture, he'd vehemently told her that she would do no such thing.

At the time she'd thought he hadn't wanted her there because he was afraid she might distract him.

She glanced around the room.

Now she was beginning to wonder if the real reason he was so opposed to her being in his class was that his students were almost all exclusively attractive young females who gazed at him with rapt attention.

Morgan let her gaze slide down his tightly muscled body. Not that she blamed them, she thought, and smiled.

If she'd had a lit professor who looked like Justin Stone when she was in college, she'd have probably hung on his every word too.

"So we realize the importance of setting when we read Faulkner," Justin was saying as he strode across the front of the auditorium. "Let's talk about emotion for a moment. It's the one ingredient to the mix that makes the reader connect with the story. Now, since everything becomes magnified in fiction, what is likely to happen with a simple love story?"

There was silence for a moment, then a female voice rang out. "It becomes all screwed up —just like in real life."

Laughter rippled through the room.

"Only worse than real life," Justin said, and grinned. "In fiction, love often turns into obsession."

He turned and walked back to the other side of the auditorium, waving his hand in the air.

"Take Fitzgerald's *The Great Gatsby*," he went on. "It was Gatsby's obsession with Daisy that drove him to succeed. It consumed him, blinding him to everything else."

A few people began to nod while others scribbled notes. He really is good at this, Morgan thought with a smile. Not that she was all that surprised by the discovery, though. Justin had always had a passion for literature, a passion he could effortlessly infuse into those around him.

And as for his current status as UCSB's "hunkiest" professor, well, his female students may have enrolled in the class because he was drop-dead gorgeous, but Morgan knew they'd stayed because he was a damn good teacher.

"The same thing is true with shorter fiction," Justin said, turning to make another trek across the front of the auditorium. His gaze swept the room. He saw Morgan and came to a complete stop, a frown tugging at the corners of his mouth.

What are you doing here? his gaze seemed to demand.

She only smiled and gave him a little wave.

He jerked his head toward the direction of the door, making it clear that he wanted her to go. *Now.*

She shook her head and mouthed "no."

"Look at E. J. Tremayne's 'Amanda in Mourning,'" Justin said, resuming his pacing.

There was a decided edge to his voice. Morgan knew he was annoyed with her, knew also that he would probably growl at her for the rest of the day about her sneaking into his class, but she didn't care. It was well worth the price of getting to see him in action.

"A young bride loses her husband on her wedding day," he said. "She trades in her wedding gown for widow's weeds and spends the next thirty years mourning for a lost love. We recognize the senselessness of her act, but we sympathize with her because Tremayne has involved our emotions."

The bell rang.

"Okay, people, that's it for this week. We'll continue the discussion next Tuesday."

A groan went through the room.

"And don't forget to mark your calendars for the symposium on American authors which starts this Monday evening. Professor Koenig's lecturing on John Steinbeck. I hope to see you all there."

"Professor Stone?" A stylishly dressed brunette raised her hand. "Are you going to tell us what the big surprise you have planned for the Tremayne workshop is? You've been keeping us in suspense all month."

A chorus of "yeah"s and "come on, professor"s filled the room.

Justin laughed. "That's why they call them

surprises, Melissa. Because you don't get to find out what they are beforehand."

"I heard E.J.'s daughter's going to be here," another female student piped in. "I bet that's it."

A few people began to murmur their consensus, while others argued it must be something else.

Morgan stared at Justin speculatively for a moment, remembering Cappy's comment at the restaurant about the "surprises" Justin had in store for the workshop. Just what was he up to? she wondered.

"Morgan's arrival was a surprise," Justin said.

He met her inquisitive gaze and actually smiled at her this time.

"Make that a big surprise," he added.

A few people twisted in their seats to stare at her.

"But I was referring to a surprise of a more historic nature," he said, tearing his gaze away. "As for what it is, well, you'll just have to show up at the symposium."

Another groan filled the air, then the students slowly began to gather their belongings and leave the room.

Justin walked back to the podium and started returning his notes to his briefcase while several young women clustered around him, bombarding him with more questions.

Morgan stood and walked down the stairs toward him.

". . . but I really think it's more of a commitment issue," an intense-looking young woman with a mop of curly red hair and thick oval glasses was saying when Morgan got within hearing range.

"I mean, in the beginning of the story the narrator was talking about changing mores, right? He said he was divorced and that things were so different now than they had been in Amanda's generation."

"Meaning?" Justin asked.

Morgan stopped next to him, catching a tantalizing whiff of his aftershave. She could feel him tense, but he didn't so much as glance in her direction.

His students eyed her curiously, though. One of them, an overweight blond in her late teens, elbowed her companion and whispered something in her ear. Then they both looked at Morgan and grinned.

"I think Tremayne's work was just mirroring his own life," the redhead said. "I mean, he wrote the story after his third divorce. Maybe he was regretting that he hadn't handled his marriages differently."

"Daddy wasn't the kind of man who believed in having regrets," Morgan said.

She reached over and straightened Justin's tie, which was slightly askew.

His fingers immediately encircled her wrist, scorching her flesh. His gaze locked with hers, a gaze filled with longing, need. She felt her heart skip a beat.

"Daddy always said you get only one chance at life," she went on, her voice dropping lower as she stared into Justin's smoke-tinged eyes. "That's why he felt you should make the most of it."

"You're Morgan Tremaync," the redhead said. "What a wild coincidence! Mind if I ask you—"

The blond student punched her friend in the arm, cutting her off in mid-request. They exchanged a whispered conference, then turned and left without another word.

Morgan doubted if Justin even noticed.

"I thought we'd agreed you were going to wait for me in my office," he said huskily.

His fingers glided along her wrist, sending waves of erotic pleasure straight down to her toes.

She sighed and leaned closer.

Then, almost as though he realized what he was doing and was none too pleased by the discovery, he pushed her hand away and took a step back.

She wanted to reach out to him, wanted to touch his arm, his chest, his face. She wanted to feel his muscles bunch and tense under her fingertips, wanted to feel the bristly stubble that shaded his cheeks rub against her hand.

Wanted especially to see the flames of desire burn brightly in his gray-green eyes again.

A desire that burned for her alone.

Instead, she shrugged and tried to look as if she were in control of her emotions.

"I changed my mind," she said. "I'd always wanted to see you teach. Now seemed the perfect opportunity."

"So what did you think?" He snapped the lid closed on his briefcase.

I think I love you, Justin Stone. I think that the biggest mistake either one of us ever made was flying to Costa Rica.

She smiled at him. "I think . . . I think you're a wonderful teacher. That your students respect you, and your love for what you do shines through."

He gave her that famous crooked smile of his. "Thanks."

"Now, what's this big surprise you've got planned for the symposium?" she asked, moving around the podium to get closer to him.

"Just that," he said. "A big surprise. And you'll have to wait and find out what it is along with everyone else."

"But I'm your wife."

"Ex-wife," he reminded her.

"Wife," she insisted. "And the daughter of the author in question."

"Sorry."

She ran her fingers lightly up his arm. "Surely

there must be some way I can drag the information out of you?"

She felt him shudder.

"Nothing whatsoever," he said. "My lips are sealed."

"Really?" she asked, moving closer. Her gaze lingered on his mouth. "That sounds awfully like a challenge, darling."

Then she leaned up and brushed her lips against his mouth. He tensed for a moment, then relaxed.

He laughed. "Shouldn't you be on your way to the children's center?" he asked, pushing her away.

He moved to the other side of the podium.

"I thought you were going to head over there this morning," he said. "Something about paperwork you needed to express down to New Orleans?"

She shrugged. "I was supposed to go over there after lunch. But I've postponed it until tomorrow morning. It seems they're having some kind of administrative crisis right now, and they asked me to reschedule."

He started walking up the stairs to the exit. She fell into step beside him.

"And you're trying to avoid my question," she told him.

Just as he was trying to avoid the desire she knew he still felt for her.

"What's this big surprise of a *historic nature* that you've got planned for the workshop?"

He grinned. "It's a surprise, Morgan."

"Justin!"

"But I will tell you this," he said. "It was something Adam Smiley found in the papers your aunt Libby donated to the university. Something . . . amazing."

Morgan frowned. She knew Aunt Libby had donated several boxes of E.J.'s personal papers to the university a couple of years before. But Morgan thought they'd just been letters and notes on the stories and novels he'd written, that kind of thing. Her father had never kept a journal, and Aunt Libby would have never donated the papers if she'd felt they included anything that might be considered historically significant.

At least, not do it and be able to keep quiet about it afterward.

"So what'd you find?" she asked, slipping her hand into the crook of his arm. "An unpublished story? Fan letters from Hemingway? What?"

"Uh-uh. Not a word will you pry out of me."

He pushed open the auditorium door, and they walked into the hall.

Morgan glanced to her right and saw Adam Smiley talking with another young man.

"Okay, fine," she said. "Be that way. I have other sources I can pump for information, you know."

She waved at Adam. "Yoo-hoo! Oh, Adam."

"You wouldn't dare," Justin muttered under his breath.

Adam returned the wave. He murmured something to his friend, then walked over to join them.

"Hi, Morgan. Justin. You guys ready for the cocktail party tomorrow night? I'm still getting goose bumps over the guest list!" he confessed with a grin. "We're talking strictly Who's Who of Southern California society here. Even a former president or two might show up."

"That's lovely," Morgan said, although she didn't really care how many notables appeared at the university's cocktail party. All she cared about was getting to the bottom of the mystery.

And she cared about *that* only because she loved teasing Justin.

"Adam, tell me about this big surprise that you and Justin have cooked up for the workshop on Daddy."

Adam glanced at Justin.

"Breathe one word . . ." Justin warned.

Adam grinned. "Sorry, Morgan. Can't help you. Besides, it's his discovery, not mine."

"Men." She rolled her eyes heavenward in mock disbelief. "You're all alike."

Justin and Adam both laughed.

But she'd get the information out of Justin, she decided. One way or another.

She tightened her grasp on his arm and grinned.

In fact, she couldn't think of a better way to spend an evening than by trying to unseal those so-called sealed lips of his.

SIX

Seven hours later, after polishing off a quick dinner of Chinese takeout, Morgan settled back on the sofa and tried to concentrate on the program notes, although the symposium was the furthest thing from her mind just then.

Who could really blame her? she wondered, shooting glances out of the corner of her eye at Justin, seated inches away from her.

He had removed his jacket so that she couldn't help but notice his broad, muscled shoulders and rock-hard chest through his thin cotton shirt.

She couldn't help but see that he'd loosened his tie—a tie she longed to reach over and grab so she could bring him closer to her.

Just as she couldn't help but remember how good it felt to make love with him for hours.

Or how his hands could stroke her body in ways that no one else ever could.

Or how his lips could kiss hers with such tenderness and feeling.

Or how . . .

"Dammit, Morgan," Justin said with a growl, "you're not even listening to me."

"Hmm?"

She looked up to meet his annoyed gaze, and flushed.

"Sorry, darling," she murmured. "I was just woolgathering. You were saying something about the press conference next week, weren't you?"

"Right, though I don't know why I even bothered if you're not going to pay attention."

"Now, Justin, don't sulk."

She gave him a smile.

"I can handle one teeny little press conference," she said, "without your getting yourself all worked up about it."

He didn't look convinced.

"I'll prepare a brief statement beforehand," she went on. "Something about how pleased I am to be there and how I have absolutely no idea what you're up to."

"Fine, but what about the cocktail party tomorrow night? We have to expect that there'll be a few reporters there."

"So? If any of them try to corner me, I'll brush them off. Besides, what could I possibly tell them? It's not as if you've decided to let me in on this big surprise of yours or anything."

She leaned over and touched his hand.

"Although you could trust me with your secret, darling," she said softly. "I wouldn't tell. No matter what kind of heinous tortures they inflicted upon me."

She stroked his fingers and felt him immediately tense.

"Nice try," he said, moving his hand away from hers. "But no deal."

He glanced at his watch. "Look, we might as well call it quits for tonight anyway. It's a few minutes before seven, and I have to be back on campus by seven-thirty for a freshman curriculum review meeting."

She grinned. "Are you sure you're going to a committee meeting and not off to meet Adam so you two can discuss the workshop on Daddy in private?"

Although she wouldn't mind all that much if he were planning such a rendezvous. It was far preferable to the fear that the committee meeting was little more than a ruse Justin had come up with to avoid spending time alone with her.

He grinned back at her. "I'm sure. Although Adam *will* be there—he has to take notes for Leonard—but we won't have time to discuss the workshop. And I don't want to catch you peering in any keyholes."

"I wouldn't want you to catch me either, darling."

"Morgan . . ."

"But you know how I get around surprises," she said. "Remember what happened with my birthday present that time?"

His green eyes darkened to a smoky gray and a flush began to color his cheeks.

"I remember," he said, his voice dropping lower. He smiled. "You nagged it out of me."

"Nagged? As I recall, I sat in your lap and kissed you for days until you finally told me."

"Same thing."

"And it was such a romantic gift, darling. The best birthday present I ever got."

It had proved that he loved her more effectively than anything else ever could.

In the early days of their marriage, they'd shared every secret, every memory, regardless of how trivial it might seem, including the fact that her favorite childhood toy had been a wooden rocking horse called Old Chester.

When she was ten, her stepmother had donated the poor old thing to a local charity, thinking Morgan wouldn't mind. Only she had. And although they'd tried, they couldn't get it back.

Then Justin decided to give it a shot. For her twenty-third birthday, he'd given her back Old Chester.

It wasn't the same rocking horse, of course. That one was long gone. But Justin had found a replacement in an antiques store in New Orleans, then spent weeks sanding it, polishing it, painting it. Trying to make it look exactly as she'd described Old Chester.

When he'd told her he had a surprise for her birthday seven days before the actual event, she'd spent the entire week seducing him, trying to make him tell her what the surprise was.

And no matter what he now said, she knew he'd loved every minute of that seduction too.

As had she.

"I still have that rocking horse, you know," she told him. "It's in my living room, right next to my fireplace."

She leaned over and traced a line down his cheek, feeling the stubble bristle beneath her fingertips. She stopped when she reached his neck. She could feel his pulse quicken, his body tense.

"Now, you know how persuasive I can be when I set my mind to it," she reminded him.

She slid her fingers around the back of his neck, feeling his hair rustle beneath her hands. She leaned closer.

"It's a secret," he said again.

"Is it really?" she asked. "You see, I can't help thinking that you want me to pry the information out of you the way I did the last time."

She pressed her lips softly against his. Once. Twice. Three times. The scent of his aftershave swam around her, making her feel dizzy.

"We really need to send you to an assertive-ness-training seminar," he said huskily.

His hands slid around her waist. His finger-tips scorched through the dress to her bare skin.

"So you can learn to communicate your needs," he murmured. He gently massaged her back.

"I thought that was what I was doing," she said.

He laughed. It was a low, throaty sound that made her insides melt like wax in a flame.

She loosened his tie. "Of course, if you'd pre-fer, I could try to be some quiet little virginal thing and wait for you to make the first move."

"Oh, no," he said in a half moan. He pulled her against him. "You're perfect just the way you are."

They slid down on the sofa.

His tongue thrust possessively into her mouth. He wove his hands through her hair and pulled her closer until her hips and thighs were aligned with his. It felt like heaven, being this close to him.

But it still wasn't close enough.

He turned on his side, taking her with him, then turned again until she was beneath him.

"Beyond perfect," he murmured against her ear. "More like some womanly ideal the poets wrote about."

"Hmm, I like that," she said.

She slowly raked her fingernails up the back of his shirt to his shoulders.

"What'd these poets say about me, you think?" she asked.

" 'O Lyric Love, half angel and half bird,' " he whispered. " 'And all a wonder and a wild desire.' "

"Robert Browning," she said, grinning. "I like it. What else?"

" 'Oh! Might I kiss those eyes of fire, a million scarce would quench desire: still would I steep my lips in bliss, and dwell an age on every kiss.' "

"Byron! Oh, God, yes! Do you know how long I've waited to hear you quote Byron to me?"

"About as long as I've waited to do this," he said huskily. He thrust his hips against hers and kissed her again.

She tugged his shirt free from the waistband of his trousers, then smoothed her hands up his back. She felt him shudder.

"Morgan, do you know what you do to me?" He groaned against her neck. "Make me so crazy with wild desire that I can't concentrate, can't work, can't do anything but think of you, of touching you, tasting you."

The unmistakable hardness of his arousal pressed firmly against her hips. Liquid heat began to pool in her lower abdomen.

"Make love to me, Justin," she said huskily.

"Make love to me, and I promise everything will be like it used to be. Only better."

Justin's hand slid down her hips to the hem of her gray sweater-dress. He tugged at the bottom and pulled it up along her inner thigh and up past her garters. The gliding of his hand along her stockinged leg sent shivers of desire tumbling down her spine.

He lightly rubbed his finger along the lacy edge of her panties.

"I've been dreaming about doing this all day," he murmured. "Sliding up that damn dress to touch your body. Even though I know it's crazy to want to do this. Absolutely insane. It's only prolonging the inevitable—"

"Oh, shut up and kiss me!"

And he did.

Quite solidly, in fact.

Then the telephone rang.

She felt him tense, and she tightened her grip on his shoulders. She arched her body to meet his until she felt him relax and the kiss deepen.

The phone rang again.

The answering machine kicked in, playing back his brief outgoing message. An electronic beep sounded, then Boyd Paul Watkins's voice boomed across the room.

"Morgan. It's Boyd Paul. Good news, honey. I talked with a friend of mine who's on the superior court down here. He's going to call a friend of his who's a judge in Los Angeles, and he ought to be able to grant the divorce soon as you and Justin sign the papers I'm drafting. I'm at home now, so why don't you give me a call when you get this message. . . ."

Morgan felt Justin pull away emotionally before his lips ever left hers. She wanted to cry out, but she knew it would do no good.

She had already lost him.

He sat up and raked his fingers through his hair.

"Justin . . . ?"

He met her gaze. She could see the desire still smoldering in his eyes, but it was a desire she now knew he would never surrender to.

"It can't be like it used to be." His voice was little more than a hoarse whisper. "It just can't."

He grabbed his jacket off the back of the sofa, picked up his briefcase, then headed for the door.

A few seconds later he was gone.

The Santa Barbara For the Children was located on a quiet tree-lined drive just off State Street. At a few minutes past three on Friday afternoon, Justin parked his Honda Accord in one of the visitor's spaces and walked into the two-story yellow and white painted building to find Morgan.

She'd gone over to the center directly after breakfast with the intention of meeting him back at the university for lunch. But she hadn't. She'd left a message for him instead, saying she was delayed and asking if he could he pick her up after his last class.

To be honest, he was glad she'd spent a few more hours at the center. As it was, he'd been haunted all day by the memory of their kiss, of how wonderful it felt to have her body pressed against his again.

Haunted by the memory of her in a black teddy, lace garters, and silk stockings.

He'd wanted her—still wanted her, in fact— with an intensity that nothing, not common sense, not all the resolutions to the contrary in the world, could dim.

It was funny, really, he thought. She'd been back in his life for only four short days, yet he knew that when she returned to New Orleans, it'd take a lifetime to get over her.

If he ever could get over her at all.

The first thing he heard when he went inside the center was children's laughter, joyous and uninhibited, echoing down the long hallway. The sparsely furnished waiting room was empty, though, except for a few well-used toys scattered about.

He looked around for a moment, then heard one of the office doors open off to his immediate right.

A middle-aged woman wearing wire-rimmed glasses and a big smile walked over to greet him.

"Hello. I'm Tricia Hunt, the center's director. How may I help you?"

"I'm Justin Stone. I'm here to—"

"Professor Stone?" Her smile grew wider. "We've been expecting you. Morgan's back in the playroom. Please, come with me."

She turned and headed off down the hall. He fell into step beside her.

"Morgan's been a real lifesaver to us today." Tricia's midsize heels tapped loudly against the worn linoleum.

"Two of our regular staffers are out with the flu," she explained. "And our receptionist has a doctor's appointment. She's expecting twins, you see—any day now," she added with a grin.

They stopped outside an unmarked door and peered in through its yellow-chintz-curtained window. Morgan sat in a semicircle on the floor with a group of children ranging in age from two to six years. Two other adults, young women in their early twenties, sat in the back of the room.

"Story time," Tricia explained. "We use it to reach some of the more withdrawn kids, to make them feel involved, part of the group."

Morgan was using hand puppets to tell a story. From the rapt look on the children's faces, he knew she had them hooked. Of course, with her voice and her father's gift for spinning a tale, it was no wonder the children were enthralled.

Just as he was every time she spoke his name.

"I only wish we could make Morgan a permanent addition to our staff," Tricia said wistfully. "She's done wonders with our center in New Orleans."

"Because of her fund-raising efforts, you mean."

"Oh, Morgan does a lot more than raise money for the center, Professor Stone," Tricia said quickly. "She raises public awareness for the plight of abused children, fights to get laws changed to protect them. Like last year, when she helped to get that legislation passed in Louisiana concerning licensing requirements for day care centers."

"What'd she do?" he asked. Morgan hadn't mentioned a word to him about winning any legislative battles.

But then, she'd never been the kind of person who advertised her accomplishments.

Tricia smiled. "What'd she do? Well, for starters, she personally called each and every congressman and senator in the state, then threatened to camp out on the governor's doorstep until the bill was pushed through. Then she spearheaded a letter-writing campaign that set new records in the state."

Tricia shook her head. "Some people sit around and wish something could be done to make the world a better place. But not Morgan Tremayne. No, she goes out and does something to make it happen. That's why she's something of a legend around here."

He watched Morgan through the window and smiled.

"A modern-day Beowulf," he murmured. "Slaying Grendels by the score."

"Excuse me?"

Tricia looked confused. She tapped on the window.

"What's a Grendel?" she asked.

Morgan turned and saw them. Her smile turned up a few degrees when she met his gaze. She said something to the children, who turned and waved at him.

He grinned and waved back.

"I meant only that Morgan is fearless," he said. "That she always has been."

While he was afraid to let himself love her again.

Four hours later Justin was pacing through his living room with his hands shoved into the pockets of his dress pants.

He had never cared much for cocktail parties, couldn't understand why anyone ever bothered to have them in the first place. He thought it was a monumental waste of time, having to get dressed up so you could mingle and make small talk with a bunch of virtual strangers who were more interested in swilling down wine and munching on cheese balls.

Unfortunately, the alumni—UCSB's primary

source of private contributions—loved cocktail parties, especially when they were kicking off a project as important to the university as the symposium on American authors.

Especially when Morgan Tremayne, the daughter of one of the country's best-loved authors, was slated to be there.

He glanced at his watch and frowned.

Provided, of course, she ever got there at all. She'd been dressing for the better part of an hour.

"Morgan," he shouted down the hall. "What's keeping you? It's already a quarter past seven. We should have been there fifteen minutes ago."

He heard the bedroom door open, followed by the soft, tinkling sound of her laughter.

"It's not funny," he called out. "We're late."

"Really, darling," she said, walking into the living room moments later. "It's only a ten-minute drive to the university. And you know that no one ever gets to these things on time. So, relax, why don't you?"

But he couldn't relax.

Hell, he couldn't even breathe.

She was wearing a black beaded dress that hugged her body so tightly, it looked as if it had been painted on her. Every curve, every gorgeous line, was emphasized and enhanced. From her firm, rounded breasts to her small waist and the gentle curve of her hips.

On most women, the dress would have merely been stylish.

On Morgan . . .

He felt his body begin to tighten again.

She met his gaze and grinned. The lights were twinkling in her eyes.

"Is something wrong, darling?" she asked.

"Is . . . that . . . what you're wearing?" he asked hoarsely.

She nodded. "What do you think?"

She did a little pirouette with her arms extended. The dress looked even better when she moved, he decided. Especially since it was cut low in the back, showing inches and inches of her smooth, tanned skin.

"This is supposed to be a university function," he reminded her. "With a lot of staid old men and middle-aged matrons. You look—"

"I look what?"

She took a step closer to him. Her perfume danced around him, making it difficult to think straight. She touched his arm, scorching through his jacket to his skin below. His mouth went dry.

"Tell me," she said. "How do I look?"

"Like you're trying to start a five-alarm fire," he muttered gruffly, and headed for the door.

"Damnation, child! You get better looking every time I see you!"

Morgan laughed and tightened her grip on

Justin's arm. "Oh, hush, Cappy. You're liable to turn a girl's head with talk like that."

They had arrived at the cocktail party a scant five minutes before. Although it was still relatively early—despite Justin's fears to the contrary —the room was already awash with sparkling designer dresses, dark suits, and high spirits.

A middle-aged couple whose name tags identified them as being members of the alumni committee walked past and nodded a greeting.

"I mean it," Cappy said. "You're by far the most beautiful woman in the room tonight. Wouldn't you agree, Justin?"

She glanced up at Justin, whose jaw was clenched so tightly, he'd probably have to pay a small fortune in dental bills before the night was over.

"Oh, don't ask him," she said. "He's already lectured me about my dress. Thinks it's too provocative for a university function."

"What?" Cappy's gaze slid down her dress and back again. "Nonsense. You look beautiful."

Cappy glanced over at a colleague who was talking with a middle-aged man in an expensive business suit. The colleague motioned for Cappy to join them.

"Ah, excuse me for a moment, dear," Cappy murmured. "Looks like it's time to charm a contribution out of a very tight wallet." Then he walked over to join his co-conspirator.

"I didn't lecture you about the dress," Justin

said, peeling her fingers off his arm. "I merely said you looked as though you were planning to start a fire."

"Well, maybe I am," she said, and grinned.

And maybe he was the one she wanted to incinerate.

She knew the knee-length cocktail dress was a little revealing—it had a modest front but practically no back at all—but that was precisely why she'd bought it.

Because the dress hugged her body so tightly, breathing became something of a luxury.

Because when she wore it, she knew she'd have Justin's undivided attention.

"I bought the dress just for you," she said. "I'm sorry you don't like it."

He retrieved two glasses of white wine from the tray of a passing waiter and handed her one. Then Justin's gaze swept slowly up and down her body, warming her to her core.

"I didn't say that I didn't like the dress," he said, his voice growing a little husky.

"Oh? Then what's the problem?"

The hint of a crooked smile played around his mouth. He glanced around the room.

"I think you know the answer to that," he said. "Besides, I thought you bought the flannel PJs for me."

"I did," she said, and took a sip of wine. "Those were for obeying your dress code, while this . . ."

"Was for starting a fire?" he asked softly.

"Something like that."

She held his gaze for a moment.

"How am I doing so far?" she asked.

She could see the passion still smoldering in his eyes. She knew he burned for her, burned with a fire whose heat could make molten lava seem cool by comparison.

But she also knew that Justin would likely fight that desire with every ounce of strength he possessed, out of nothing else but sheer stubbornness.

He frowned. "Morgan . . ."

"You see, I was thinking," she said, leaning closer. She glided her fingers down the front of his shirt to his belt.

"That maybe for one night," she went on, "like tonight, we didn't have to be married or divorced or anything at all."

She stroked the hard leather for a moment, then slid her fingers back up his chest.

"That we didn't have to be Justin and Morgan with a history so long, the transcript could fill a library."

"So who did you want us to be?" he asked.

He grasped her wrist and pressed the palm of her hand against his chest.

"Scarlett and Rhett?"

"If you'd like," she said.

He smiled. "So I could sweep you into my arms and carry you up a winding staircase to make mad, passionate love to you all night long? Is that the general idea?"

A flush crept into her cheeks. That was *precisely* the general idea, she thought.

"Why not?" she asked. "You see, I was thinking that maybe, just for tonight, we wouldn't have to be ourselves. We could just be a man and a woman with no past, no future, only a brief moment of time together."

She slid her hand out of his grasp and grabbed his tie. She gave it a yank, and he leaned closer.

"I'm offering you the chance of a lifetime, darling," she said softly. "A chance to flirt outrageously with your ex-wife without any repercussions. A chance to follow through on every mad impulse you feel for me without fear. A chance to fulfill your fantasies . . . and mine . . . with no strings attached. But you'd better act quickly."

She gave him a kiss on his chin. "You see, the offer's good only for tonight."

Then she turned and walked away.

SEVEN

Justin downed his glass of wine and quickly glanced around for another.

Morgan stood across the room, engrossed in a conversation with Will Petersen and Otto Koenig, two of the four other lit professors working with Justin on the symposium.

She was laughing at something one of the men said. Her head was tilted back, her eyes were sparkling, her face glowing. Each supple movement of her body made the black beads on her skin-tight dress shimmer under the fluorescent lights.

Each supple movement of her body made the want for her grow stronger inside him.

Justin couldn't stop himself from wondering what she had on underneath it, if she was wearing the garter belt again and those silk stockings.

He also couldn't stop thinking about what

she'd said to him, about how they should forget reality and lose themselves in a fantasy for a night. She'd made the offer so matter-of-factly, as though one night with her would ever be enough.

As though he could make love with her again and not lose his soul in the process.

She glanced in his direction. Her gaze locked with his, then she flirted with him for a moment, flashing a smile his way that fanned the fire inside him to a near-raging inferno.

He took a step toward her, feeling sort of like a moth drawn into a flame. He knew it would be the death of him, but he was powerless to resist.

"Hi, Justin!" Adam struck him on his back. "Some turnout, huh?"

"What?" Justin blinked at Adam as though he'd suddenly started speaking ancient Greek.

"The turnout," Adam said, beaming. "Pretty impressive, huh? You'll never believe who I just met," he added, dropping his voice lower.

"What?" Justin asked again.

"Delores Zwitek," Adam explained. "You know, the director everyone's sure will win the Academy Award this year? She's really nice too. I told her all about this screenplay I've been working on. She thought I should send it to an agent friend of hers."

Justin mumbled something that he hoped was intelligible if not appropriate, then glanced over to where Morgan had been standing.

She was gone.

Frowning, he scanned the room. He finally found her near the bar, encircled by Otto, Will, and six new admirers, looking for all the world like Scarlett with her beaus waiting for Rhett to send them scattering.

She met his gaze and grinned. Challenging him. Daring him to come after her.

His desire for her became an aching need.

A waiter walked past with another tray of wine. Justin gave the waiter his empty glass and took a new goblet, which he promptly downed before returning the empty glass to the tray.

The wine didn't help. His throat still felt parched and his nerves still felt as if they were stretched to their breaking points.

"Have you told her yet?" Adam asked.

"Huh?"

Justin glanced at Adam, surprised to find him still there.

"Told who what?" Justin asked.

"Told Morgan about the manuscript of her father's that we uncovered."

Justin shook his head. "Not yet."

He'd wanted to wait until the actual day of the press conference, if possible, before breaking the news. That they'd found an original hand-written E. J. Tremayne manuscript in the boxes of papers donated to the university by her aunt Libby. That they'd found a copy of "Summer Heat," in fact, the short story for which E.J. had won his Pulitzer.

The find would likely be the literary discovery of the decade, if not the century.

Everyone knew E.J. preferred to write his stories out in longhand first before having them transcribed, after which he destroyed the original draft. For some reason, though, he'd saved "Summer Heat" and hid it in the back of a tattered copy of Mark Twain's *Tom Sawyer*. The handwritten manuscript even had E.J.'s revisions scribbled in its margins.

Justin knew how Morgan would react to the news of the discovery. She had once told him that she believed her father had destroyed his first drafts because he felt the published work didn't deserve all the accolades heaped upon them, that he'd thought he was a hack and only Faulkner deserved the title of writer.

She'd also told Justin that she'd wished E.J. had saved the handwritten drafts. That since she'd been too young to watch him write them, reading his first draft would have been the next best thing.

Justin had sworn to Morgan that he'd do everything in his power to find one of her father's original manuscripts, if one still existed.

As it turned out, it was the only promise he'd ever made to Morgan that he'd managed to keep.

He watched her tuck a strand of hair behind her ear. The simple gesture caused something to snap inside him like an earthen dam giving way to the power of a tidal wave.

Suddenly, he didn't care about the dictates of common sense or logic or anything else. All he cared about was holding her again. Touching her. Caressing her. And not just for one night either.

Hell, eternity wouldn't be long enough.

He started walking toward her.

Morgan felt her heart begin to pound and her stomach do a somersault as she watched Justin make his way across the crowded room toward her.

A part of her—the part that was still sane enough to realize that what she was doing was crazy—told her she should end the charade now, while she still could. That one night with Justin with no strings attached would only break her heart into a million pieces.

But the other part of her, the part that was in control, didn't care one whit about the consequences. She loved him, loved him with every fiber of her being. But with the barriers he'd thrown up around himself, she knew it might take only one night in each other's arms to remind him that he still cared for her too.

In fact, the way she saw it, one night together might be the only chance she ever had of winning him back.

Otto smiled and handed her another glass of Chablis. "Morgan, would you care for a—?"

"Excuse me," she murmured, and brushed

past him to meet Justin in the middle of the room.

They stared at each other for a moment, standing just inches apart, though it seemed to her as if miles separated them.

She was dimly aware of voices around them, of snatches of conversation, laughter, even of someone calling her name. Soon, though, everything began to fade except for Justin's face.

She felt as though his gaze were burning its way into her soul.

"Hello," she said finally, wondering if she sounded as breathless as she felt. "I don't believe we've met. I'm—"

"Morgan Tremayne."

His voice was a husky whisper that made her knees feel weak.

"And I'm Justin Stone." He traced a fingertip down her cheek to her chin.

She wanted to lean against him, wanted to feel his arms around her again.

She smiled. "But I thought we were going to be Scarlett and Rhett," she said. "As in winding staircases and mad, passionate love. As in—"

"And I thought I told you last night," he said, placing his finger over his lips, "that you're perfect just the way you are." He glided his fingers around her jaw to touch her hair. "I wouldn't want you to be anyone but yourself."

"But . . ."

He leaned down and kissed her, gently brushing his lips against hers, sending one shiver after another racing down her spine until she softly moaned.

"You're the only fantasy I've ever had," he whispered against her ear sometime later. "The only fantasy I *could* ever have. You're the one I've dreamed about every night for nearly six years, the only one whose face I see every time I close my eyes."

She slid her arms under his jacket and around his waist. "Sometimes I feel like I'm simply going to melt when you talk to me like that," she said huskily.

"You're the one who said she wanted to start a five-alarm fire," he reminded her.

Then he pulled her closer and kissed her again, deeper this time. The kind of kiss a man would give a woman when they're all alone.

The kind of kiss that she knew would be sheer madness to initiate when you're in a room full of your colleagues, alumni committee members, Board of Regents, and the occasional reporter or two.

But it seemed to her that Justin was past caring about keeping his private life private, even though she was sure their behavior would likely cause a mini scandal on campus the following day.

As if to prove her point, she heard someone gasp and a female voice murmur "Oh, my." They even got a few rounds of applause.

She reluctantly pulled away to stare up at Justin. All he did was smile at her.

"Come on," he said, and slid his hand around her waist. "Let's get out of here."

Then they headed for the door.

It took them less than ten minutes to drive to Justin's apartment, yet it seemed to Morgan to be the longest ten minutes of her life.

She kept casting furtive glances out of the corner of her eye at him the whole time, wondering if he now regretted kissing her at the cocktail party in front of his friends and colleagues, wondering if he'd changed his mind about making love to her.

She didn't have the courage to ask him either question, though.

She was too afraid of what his answer might be.

When they walked into the living room, he tossed his keys onto the small rattan table next to the door, then eased the door closed and dropped the deadbolt into place.

"Why don't I get us a drink," she suggested, starting to walk past him. "I think I saw a bottle of brandy in your cupboard."

"I don't need it," Justin said, pulling her into his arms. "You're all the stimulation I can handle."

His tongue slid into her mouth, seeking out

hers. And he kissed her. Slowly. Deeply. Until she felt as if her knees would buckle. Until she knew that thoughts of campus gossip, of pushing her away, were the last things on his mind.

His hands slid down to her hips. He began to massage her buttocks, pulling her closer against the length of him, molding her to him until she felt she would likely go stark raving mad just from the want of him.

"It feels like somebody had to pour you into this dress," he whispered in her ear. "Or maybe it was shrink-wrapped with you inside. Either way, it's been driving me crazy all night, the way it hugs your body in all the places I want to hug."

His hands slid up to caress the exposed skin of her back. His touch sent a shiver coursing through her.

"And I thought you didn't like it," she said breathlessly. "The dress, I mean."

He chuckled softly. "Oh, I like the dress, Morgan. I like how it looks on you, how it shimmers every time you move. But I think I'd like how you look out of it even better."

His fingers reached for the zipper on her left side. He tugged down on the tab slowly, one excruciating quarter-inch at a time. It was torture, sheer torture, the way his fingertips burned her skin through the zippered opening, making her quiver from his touch, setting her nerve endings aflame and her senses reeling. Such sweet torture just from the exquisite slowness of it.

She wanted him to go faster, wanted him to strip off her clothes, then his, until there was nothing standing between them except bare, fevered skin. She wanted it so badly, she couldn't understand why he didn't share her impatience.

His lips brushed against hers. Lightly. Teasingly. Then he licked her lips with the tip of his tongue as his mouth kissed hers. He did it again. And again. Until she couldn't take it anymore.

Groaning, she wound her fingers in his hair and pulled him closer, forcing her tongue into his mouth to seek his, begging him to give her what she wanted, what she needed—dozens of his lazy, bone-melting kisses, the kind of kisses she'd been craving for the past six years.

The kind of kisses she'd begun to fear she'd never enjoy again.

She leaned closer, until the warmth of his body heat enveloped her, closer still until she felt the power of his arousal pressing against her abdomen.

She felt so in tune with him, so positively in sync, she could swear she felt the erratic beating of his heart as acutely as she did her own, swear she felt the blood pounding through his veins.

"Oh, Justin, please."

She wasn't sure what she was asking him for, didn't know whether it was his hands or lips or entire body she needed most just then. All she knew was that she wanted him, wanted as much of him as he could give.

For as long as she could take it.

He tilted her head back to kiss her neck, making her skin sizzle with each slow brush of his lips, with each delicious rake of his tongue.

"Please what?" he asked huskily. "Please do this?"

He slid the tip of his tongue along the edge of her ear, then gently nibbled on her lobe until a low moan came from deep inside her throat. Pleasure ricocheted through her, pure and uncensored.

"Or please do this?" he asked.

Sliding his hand back down to her buttocks to brace her, he started to move his hips against hers in a slow, sensuous circular motion that nearly drove her over the edge. He was hard. So hard. And she wanted him so badly, she began to ache for him.

"Yes . . . oh, yes!"

"Which? What do you want me to do, Morgan? Tell me."

She stared into his passion-filled eyes for a moment. Was he honestly expecting her to choose between pleasures? She shook her head.

He squeezed her buttocks again, pulling her against him. "Or maybe what you really want," he said, brushing his face against her hair, "is for me to whisper passages from Shelley and Byron in your ear all night long."

She groaned again—*Byron!*—and arched her body to meet the circular thrust of his. She felt as if she were on fire, burning with a flame that could never be extinguished. Her senses were on overload. It was too much. Didn't he realize what he was doing to her?

"Yes." She moaned. "I want poetry. And I want your hands and your tongue. I want every part of you. I want you to make love to me with beautiful words as well as with your body. I want it all, Justin. And I want it *now.*"

He laughed. "Soon," he said. "Soon. I promise."

His voice seemed ragged around the edges, as though his self-control were rapidly slipping away.

He eased his hand into the zippered opening of her dress to caress her skin, to brand her with his fingertips, claim her for his own, gently stroking her until she squirmed. The dress was still a tight fit, though, and his range of motion was limited. He tugged at the dress for a moment, trying to get it off her, then finally stopped.

"I think this thing should have come with instructions," he murmured against her ear.

Laughing, she pulled away and undid the halter clasp at the base of her neck with shaking fingers. Then she helped him pull the dress off her shoulders and down past her knees, until it landed in a crumpled heap at her feet. She stepped out of both the dress and her high heels.

He stared at her for a moment, letting his smoke-tinged gaze slide slowly down her body, stoking the flames inside her even hotter. She was naked except for her black lace panties, her garter belt, and silk stockings. The dress had been so form-fitting there'd been no need to wear a bra.

"You're so beautiful," he said.

He reached over and touched her breasts. A shudder rippled through her.

She felt her nipples begin to harden. Then a languid, sensual heat swamped her, leaving her utterly weak, unable to breathe, before it settled in her loins—where she burned for him.

"So beautiful that no poem could ever do you justice," he whispered. "So beautiful that no mere words could ever begin to describe you. I just want to touch you, Morgan. Taste you. And never stop."

She closed her eyes for a moment, reveling in the feel of his masterful hands on her body as he stroked her, caressed her, rejoicing in the damp warmth of his tongue against her breasts and the gentle rake of his teeth on her sensitized nipples. He was taking what he wanted from her as if he were the pirate she'd once teased him of being.

She opened her eyes as he slid his hands down her hips to the black lace garter. She watched as he knelt down and carefully unsnapped each clasp, releasing the silk stocking. Then he kissed her inner thigh gently, so gently. His lips scorched her skin.

She gasped, certain her knees would buckle, but by some miracle they didn't. Then his tongue began to lick her feverish skin, moving in small concentric circles that sent thousands of white-hot shivers cascading down her spine.

"I've been dreaming about these garters since I saw you wearing them the other morning," he said, kissing her thigh again. "You got these for me, didn't you? Just like the dress. Just like those damn flannel pajamas."

"Yes."

Her voice was little more than a strangled cry.

"I bought them all for you. I—I remembered how you used to love to see me in garter belts and stockings."

He laughed. "I used to love getting you *out* of garter belts and stockings, or don't you remember that?"

How could she forget? It had been part of their seduction ritual, a ritual it had taken them many pleasure-filled months to perfect. First, she'd slowly dress in the black lace garter belt, silk stockings, and black silk teddy as he watched; then he'd undress her, removing the clothes with the same excruciating slowness.

An excruciating slowness he seemed intent upon repeating now.

He slid the garter belt down her hips and let it fall to the floor. Then, with a deliberate leisureliness, he rolled down the stocking on her right leg, sliding the tips of his fingers, first along her thigh with a featherlike touch, then along her calf. His lips and tongue followed the trail, kissing and licking her mid-thigh, then her knee, her calf, her ankle.

She shivered again from the sensual on-slaught. He was trying to drive her insane, she decided. And she thought she knew why. It was to make her pay for teasing him so unmercifully the past four days.

Bracing her hand against his shoulder, she trembled as she lifted her foot and let him draw off the stocking. He cradled her foot in his palm for a moment, then kissed her sole, raking his tongue along the tender flesh until she knew she'd collapse on the floor beside him.

"Justin, please, I can't take much more of this."

He looked up and smiled that crooked smile of his. It made her heart so full, she thought it would burst.

"But you said you wanted all of me." He started to massage her toes between his thumb and forefinger. "You said you wanted my hands and my tongue, every part of me. And I promised to give it to you."

He gingerly lowered her foot to the carpet-ing, then repeated the sweet torture with her other stocking. This time he even kissed her toes.

Setting her foot back down, he slid his hands up her legs to her hips. He slipped his fingers under the lacy edge of her panties. Then he pressed his lips against the silky fabric, wetting her with his tongue. She moaned, thrusting her hips toward his mouth.

Dear God, what was he doing to her? she wondered. Her throat constricted; her ears thudded from the pounding of her heart as his tongue teased her. She swallowed hard. Although she'd never swooned before in her life, she felt quite certain she was about to start.

She reached down for him, but he pushed her hands away. Then he tugged her panties down her hips, his fingernails gently raking her goosepimply flesh, until they dropped to the floor at her feet. He lifted each foot out of the silk, then stroked her ankles one last time before standing.

She was incinerating, she thought. Being consumed by fire from the inside out.

She slid her hands up his chest. His cotton shirt was cool against her warm palms. But she didn't want to feel his clothes. No, she wanted to feel his bare skin, wanted to feel the heat of him against her, inside her.

She grappled with his jacket, helping him shrug it off. It landed on the floor next to her dress. He pried off his loafers and kicked them aside.

Her fingers trembled as she undid his tie, slipping the silk swatch of fabric out of its knot and letting it slide down to the floor. She wanted—no, needed—to touch him, to stroke his tightly muscled body just as he'd stroked her.

But Justin forced her to wait a few agonizing minutes longer.

He kissed the hollow of her neck. His hands palmed her breasts, squeezing the stiffened peaks between his thumbs and forefingers, bringing wave after wave of pleasure crashing around her, bringing murmurs of delight gasping from her lips.

Then he whispered snippets of poetry in her ear, just as he'd promised. It was John Donne this time. Something about licensing his hands to roam. It made her laugh, and then the hunger assailed her again, the all-consuming need for him.

She tugged his shirt out of his trousers and fumbled with the buttons. Her fingers felt numb, useless. Try as she might, she couldn't seem to get the buttons undone.

"Darling, I can't . . ."

His fingers slid over hers. He grabbed the edges of his shirt and ripped it open, sending buttons flying in every direction.

He tugged off the shirt and tossed it aside, then reached for her again. He tilted her chin up to his face and kissed her with the same hunger, with the same soul-shaking need that she felt for him. She groaned and leaned against him for support.

His skin felt feverish, as hot to the touch as hers. She eased her hand down his bare chest, feeling the tightly corded muscles of his abdomen undulate beneath her fingers, sliding her way down to his pants, where she cradled the growing bulge there in her palm. She stroked him, caressed him, until she heard him softly moan.

She stroked him, caressed him, until she felt the shudder ripple through him, until she heard the soft hiss of his sucked-in breath. She marveled at the power she had over him, felt giddy with it. Touching him this way made her feel wilder, more wanton than she'd ever been before.

She fumbled with the belt with her other hand, then eased it undone. She unzipped his trousers. He helped her pull both them and his boxer shorts down past his hips, down past his hardness. Then he peeled off the clothes and socks and tossed them toward the sofa.

She felt her breath catch in her throat as she stared at the sight of his fully aroused body. He was even more magnificent than she'd remembered. She reached out and touched him.

Groaning, he pushed her against the frigid coolness of the wall and kissed her, thrusting his tongue into her mouth with a fierceness that took her breath away. The satiny warmth of his shaft pressed against her abdomen. She started to tremble. It had been so long since they'd been together like this, she thought.

Too long.

He slid his hand between her legs, spreading her apart as the kiss deepened. He slipped a finger inside her. Liquid heat began to swirl, a heat that only he could cool. She arched herself toward him. Then he started to touch her with the same deliberate slowness he'd used when he'd removed her stockings and panties. He eased his finger out, then thrust it back inside her, stretching deep into her wetness, probing her secrets again and again, until all she could do was writhe in pleasure and murmur his name.

God, she was ready for him. So ready, she felt she would explode if he didn't enter her.

As though sensing her need, he pressed her back against the wall. She opened her mouth to accept his tongue, opened her body to accept him. Then he entered her with a single hard thrust that made her cry out from its sheer carnal beauty. She wrapped her arms around his shoulders and held on as he thrust into her again. And again.

They made love feverishly, just as they had the first time in her father's office, as though they couldn't get enough of each other, no matter how hard they tried.

Her heart was pounding, her mouth felt dry. She could feel the fireburst rapidly building inside her. She wanted to make the pleasure last, but she had been too long without him.

"Justin . . . oh, Justin!"

"I could quote you a thousand love poems," he murmured hoarsely, "and they'd never compare with the poetry we're making right now. You feel so good, Morgan. So damn good. And the way you squeeze me." He groaned. "God, you're going to milk me dry."

She cried out his name, pressing her fingertips into the rock-hard muscles of his shoulder as the pleasure washed over her in waves. Then she felt Justin's release overtake him.

She tightened her hold on him, drawing him deeper inside her. Needing him deeper.

Her mouth reached for his again. She kissed him, holding him tight, keeping him locked in her embrace until his passion was spent.

He stayed locked inside her until, utterly exhausted, they both slid down to the floor, where they clung to each other until the trembling stopped.

EIGHT

Justin knew he'd made a mistake.

Lying on the floor with Morgan's head resting on his shoulder, her arm linked around his waist, he stared up at the ceiling as his fever for her began to cool. He should have tried harder to resist the desire, he told himself in self-recrimination.

He should have thought with his head and not with his body and his heart.

But it had felt so good making love with her. Better than the first time had been. God, when he held her in his arms, he hadn't cared about anything else because nothing else had mattered. She was the sun, the center of his solar system, and he was caught in her gravitational pull, gladly careening toward spontaneous combustion.

She began to stir. "Tell me something, darling," she murmured, tracing a path down his abdomen with her fingers. "Do you think that when we're both very old, we'll make love in a bed like normal people?"

She reached lower, past his hips, until she could touch him, until she could cradle him in her warm palm. Then she started to caress him ever so gently, like the soft brushes of a feather.

He sighed and closed his eyes for a moment, concentrating on the sensations she was unleashing inside him, amazed by the fire she was building within him again.

"Or do you think we'll be chasing each other in our walkers all through the nursing home," she went on. "Giving the staff fits. Causing scandals right and left as they catch us making love in the sunroom or garden or wherever else the spirit may move us."

His body tightened, grew harder as her strokes became bolder, more erotic. His skin sizzled and burned as her fingers worked their sensual magic on him. He sighed at the wonder of it and opened his eyes.

"I think a passion this hot can never be cooled," he said, slowly exhaling. "No matter how much time passes."

"Never?" she asked.

She wrapped her fingers around the length of him and began to squeeze, gently massaging him into full erectness.

He groaned and covered her hand with his,

pressing her palm against him, showing her how he wanted it to feel.

"Never," he whispered hoarsely.

And how could it when she could send him spiraling out of control with one stroke of her hand?

It was incredible, he thought, simply incredible how nothing else mattered except touching her or being touched by her, how, just as before, he didn't want to think about the consequences.

He wanted only to experience the joy, the magic of loving her.

He lowered his head to kiss her, savoring the sweet taste of her mouth, luxuriating in the sensual feel of her tongue moving against his. He could kiss her for hours and never grow tired of it.

He slid his hand away from hers and brought it slowly up her body, skimming lightly over her smooth, silky skin until he reached her breast. He felt her nipple grow taut beneath his manipulating fingers, heard the sigh escape her as their kiss deepened.

He knew she felt the same hunger he did, felt the same all-consuming need. As much as they'd had of each other, it still wasn't enough.

Something told him it never would be.

He shifted slightly so that she was lying on the carpet rather than against his shoulder. Then he eased her hand away from him. He wanted the pleasure of loving her to last for as long as it could. He knew that if she continued to touch him the way she'd been doing, it would likely be over before it even got started again.

"I think we'll do more than cause a scandal in a nursing home," he said huskily, gliding his hand past the curve of her hip.

He reached for her other breast, palming the creamy mound in his hand, stroking her until the soft skin puckered and its tip became rigid.

"I think we'll inspire a whole generation of lovers," he said.

"Hmm," she murmured, arching her back slightly. "I like the sound of that. Tell me more, darling."

He smiled. Her nipples had hardened into little peaks of rose-tipped pleasure that he longed to taste. He leaned down and licked his tongue across a hardened nub, then pulled it into his mouth. He caressed the peak with his tongue, raked it with his teeth. He molded it, reshaped it with his mouth, until her fingers grabbed his hair, until she moaned softly and arched her body to meet his assault on her senses.

"Tell me," she said breathlessly. "How . . . how would we inspire them?"

"How?"

He slowly raised his head. Her face was flushed with passion, her breasts damp and reddened from the mark of his mouth.

She looked so beautiful, he thought, feeling a

pang of longing that had little to do with sexual desire.

He swallowed hard.

"You see," he said, knowing his voice had gone ragged around the edges again. "They'll come down to the rest home, all these young lovers. And they'll point to us and say, 'Would you look at that. He'll be ninety years old this June. And he still can't keep his hands off her.'"

As if to demonstrate what he meant, he slid his hands over her breasts, caressing them, molding them against his palm.

Her gaze locked with his. "'Still can't keep his hands off his wife,'" she corrected hoarsely. "That's what they'll say, darling. That he can't keep his hands off his wife."

He felt a muscle tighten around his heart.

"His wife," he repeated. *"My wife."*

"Your wife. Forever."

No, he thought, and squeezed his eyes closed. Not forever. Only for a few more days. Only until the divorce papers were signed and the final decree given by the judge in Los Angeles. He had to remember that.

He felt her hand reach past his hips to stroke him again. Bringing him to the edge, testing the limits of his control. Touching him and caressing him until he pushed the emotional pain to some dark recess of his mind and opened his eyes.

Then he kissed her with a frenzy, kissed her

as though he'd never get another chance to kiss her again.

His hand slid down her body to the mound of soft black curls just above her thighs. He slipped his fingers inside her, feeling the shudder that coursed through her as he began to stroke her.

He rubbed his thumb across her tightened nub of desire. Softly at first. Then harder. He wanted to take her to the top of the mountain and then home again, wanted to burn the memory of the moment into their souls forever.

"Oh, Justin." She moaned. "I can't wait anymore. I need to feel you inside me. Now."

And he needed to feel himself lost inside of her.

He reached for her mouth again. And as the kiss deepened, he eased himself into her warmth, surrendered himself to their passion.

Sunlight streaming through the white wooden slats of Justin's bedroom window woke Morgan shortly before ten the next morning. She stretched slowly, feeling her tight muscles ache in delicious protest, and smiled as the memories of their night together came flooding back.

Memories of Justin's mouth on hers and of his hands stroking her, caressing her.

Memories especially of his hard, muscled body loving her until they both swore they couldn't move, until they'd stumbled into his bedroom, where they drifted off to sleep wrapped tightly in each other's arms.

"Good morning, darling."

She spoke in a low, husky murmur that she hoped awakened the same memories in him.

"Just in case I didn't mention it to you last night, you were . . ."

She rolled over and found only emptiness.

". . . fabulous."

She sat up and glanced around. Justin was gone. Long gone by the looks of it.

A folded sheet of paper lay propped on the nightstand with her name written across it in black ink.

Frowning, she reached for the note. She flipped it open and read Justin's familiar scrawl:

> *Have gone back to campus to finish grading papers. Didn't want to wake you. Dinner at six at the Harbor Restaurant? J.*
> *P.S.: Yes, I know it's Saturday.*

Smiling again, she drew up her legs under the cream-and-tan-colored comforter and rested her chin on her knees.

Poor darling, she thought. He was at it again.

Hightailing it for safety rather than admitting what he felt for her.

She sighed. Didn't he realize it was too late to play it safe now?

Much too late.

❦————————————❦

Morgan spent the day at the center, helping out in the playroom. Working with the kids took all of her energy, all her concentration, and it gave her little time to dwell on Justin.

Just as sitting in the bar at the Harbor Restaurant at six that evening, waiting for him to show up, gave her more than ample time to remember every moment from the night before.

She felt as nervous as a teenager on a first date. Her palms were damp, her pulse racing, her stomach was all in knots.

The previous night, everything had been wonderful between them. Better than wonderful. Better even than the first time, when all they'd known was the joys of love and not its heartache.

And that morning . . .

She sighed and twirled the straw in her glass of sparkling water.

And that morning he'd sneaked out like a coward while she slept.

They both knew he could have graded the papers at home as easily as at his office.

They both knew his going to the university was only another ruse to avoid being alone with her, only another barrier he'd thrown up to keep them apart.

She took a sip of her drink and glanced at the door again. Justin stood in the doorway, scanning the bar. She caught his gaze and waved. He nodded and started toward her.

Her heart skipped a beat as she watched him maneuver his way through the tables. She really did love him, she thought with a stab of longing.

Even more now than she had six years earlier.

"Hello, darling," she murmured.

She slid off the barstool and leaned up to give him a kiss.

She felt him tense, but he didn't pull away. The kiss he gave her, though, was strictly perfunctory. No passion, no emotion. It was more like the kiss you'd give a distant relative at a family reunion than the kiss you'd give a woman you'd made love passionately with the night before.

If he'd punched her in the face, it couldn't have hurt her more.

He avoided looking directly at her.

"I think our table's ready," he said, glancing around. "Unless you'd rather finish your drink first . . ."

"Ah, no. I'm fine."

She grabbed her purse and followed him back through the bar into the restaurant.

They didn't get the same table they'd had before, although it had the same breathtaking view of the marina. She even carefully perused Justin as he read his menu, just as she'd done the last time they'd been there.

Only now she didn't like what she saw.

He'd done more than throw up barriers, she realized, feeling her insides grow cold.

He'd erected a high security quarantine around his heart that would make Fort Knox's security measures seem laughable by comparison.

When the waiter arrived, Justin ordered a lobster bisque for them both. After they were poured iced tea, they sat back in their chairs and made a lot of small talk. They discussed her work at the center, the chances the Dodgers had of winning the pennant race during the following summer, whether John Grisham's books were as good as everyone swore they wore.

When they touched on the weather, she decided she'd had enough.

"I promised you no repercussions, darling," she said quietly.

She reached across the table and took his hand. It felt cold, so she gently chafed his skin with her palm to warm him.

"And I *meant it*," she added.

He flushed. He slid his hand out of hers and reached for his iced tea.

"I don't know what you're talking about," he said.

"Of course you do," she murmured, trying to sound as though his rejection didn't devastate her nearly as much as it did.

"I'm talking about last night," she went on. "About us. I told you at the cocktail party that we could spend the night together without any obligation on your part. That we could be perfect strangers who share only one night if that's what you wanted. I'm not going to try to change the terms of our agreement now, so you can relax."

And even though her heart felt as if it would simply shatter, she didn't regret making him the offer either.

In fact, she would make it again if she thought it would give her one more chance to win his heart.

"I know what you said, Morgan," he said quietly.

He stared down into his iced tea and frowned.

"And I know what I said," he went on. "What we did. I don't need you to absolve me of my share of the responsibility in this."

She tried to smile although it felt as though her cheeks were too numb to move.

"You make it sound like we knocked over a bank or something. All we did was make love."

Wonderfully glorious love, she thought.

The kind of love he'd said that no poem by Shelley or Byron could ever compare with.

She reached for Justin's hand again. "I know I've made no secret of the fact that I would like to try for a reconciliation, but I said no strings and I meant no strings."

He scowled. "You make it sound so easy. As if I can just cut off my emotions like a light switch. But I can't, Morgan. I can't pretend that I don't feel the things I do when you touch me. And I can't pretend that what happened last night didn't have strings attached. The kind of strings I don't want."

He met her gaze. "The kind of strings that not even you can release me from."

"Then why pretend at all?" she asked. "Why not just follow your heart? One more chance, darling, that's all we really need."

"Dammit, Morgan, you know a reconciliation wouldn't work. It'd just be a repeat of what happened six years ago."

"Who says what happened six years ago was all that bad?"

She stroked his hand, drawing tiny erotic circles with her fingertip along the edge of his wrist and over his thumb.

"It wasn't all bad, but there were parts . . ." He sighed. "Do you remember my American lit lecture? The one you sat in on the other day?"

She nodded. "And I thought you were wonderful. Your students hung on your every word."

"I was talking about obsession. About how it can blind a person to everything around him. The way Gatsby was with Daisy. The way I am with you."

He moved his hand out of her grasp, then pressed his palm to hers, interlocking their fingers.

"We were obsessed with each other when we were married," he said softly. "Oblivious of everything else except our desire. But when our passion finally cooled enough for rational thought to return, I think we both realized that we were from two completely different worlds, that our lives were destined to head in two different directions."

She shook her head. "I never thought that. Only you did. I thought we were a perfect match. Still do."

He stared at her for a moment. "So why do you think we split up?"

She rubbed her thumb gently along the ridge of his.

"Because we were too young mostly," she said. "Because you were an out-of-work newlywed trying to finish your doctoral dissertation, because it kept you frazzled, nearly exhausted from trying to juggle all your responsibilities. Because I was too immature to know what I wanted to be when I grew up."

She smiled. "But we've changed, Justin. Both of us have. Now you're an associate professor about to be offered tenure. And I've got a wonderful job that I love. Can't you see?" she asked, squeezing his hand. "We're both ready to make a commitment to a relationship now, where we probably weren't ready before."

"Maybe," he said, disengaging his hand from hers. "But that still doesn't alter—"

"And besides," she said, refusing to let him

sidetrack her. "Six years ago our biggest problem wasn't the fact that we came from different worlds. It was money. You were so stubborn—no, make that absolutely pigheaded—about not using any of mine to pay our bills. You insisted on taking care of our expenses all by yourself, even though you didn't have the financial resources to care for a hamster, let alone two people. Even though a marriage is supposed to be a partnership."

His jaw began to stiffen. "I told you when I married you that I didn't care about your money. That I wanted you, not the Tremayne fortune."

"But when you rejected my money, you rejected me. You never understood that my having money was simply a part of my life, along with Daddy's books and Aunt Libby's pecan pies. That it was no big deal."

She leaned back in her chair. "Do you remember that last big fight we had?"

He shrugged.

"Well, I do," she said. "The rent on that old farmhouse we'd leased was two months past due, and we were being threatened with eviction. I withdrew some money from my trust fund to take care of it, and you went absolutely ballistic on me. Said you didn't need me to carry you. It was the first really big fight we ever had—and the last. We flew to Costa Rica three days later."

He frowned. "I acted like an idiot about that,

I admit it. But I didn't want to be accused of riding along on the Tremayne coattails any more than I already had."

"So you decided to go to the other extreme," she said. "You decided you could make it on your own without any help from anybody, including your own wife."

"Like I said, I acted like an idiot."

He reached for his iced tea and took a long swallow. He was quiet for a moment, then went on.

"I know you've wondered why I never told Leonard about us. The truth is, when I first applied for the position, I didn't want him to think that I was trying to trade in on E.J.'s name. I wanted to make it or not on the strength of my own credentials, my own hard work. Then the years sort of passed and there didn't seem to be much point in telling him."

She smiled. "Well, I've got a news flash for you, darling. People already know we were married. Your assistant, Sonia, told me she's seen that photograph you keep of us in your desk. And Cappy's known all along. He said Aunt Libby wrote him years ago about us."

"Really?" Justin shook his head and grinned. "That makes sense, I guess. Considering some of the comments Sonia's let slip. As for Leonard, well, he came by my office today when I was grading papers. Told me the cocktail party last night was a huge success, everyone's hyped about the symposium, especially your participation."

He swirled the tea, making the ice cubes tinkle against the heavy glass.

"He, ah, said he'd seen us leave early and wondered if it meant I'd finally come to my senses."

The waiter came back to the table then with their food. Morgan felt as if she were sitting on pins and needles as she waited for him to serve the lobster bisque and refill their iced tea glasses so they could be alone again.

Once the waiter turned to leave, she leaned forward.

"And have you?" she asked breathlessly. "Come to your senses, I mean?"

Justin met her gaze. She saw the shadow of pain cross his face and she knew what his answer would be.

"Morgan, I . . ." he began, then slowly shook his head. "I'm sorry."

"It's okay, darling," she said, leaning back. She waved her hand in the air as though it didn't matter.

"We can talk about this later," she said. "Now eat your dinner before it grows cold."

She was certain she couldn't eat a bite, though. There was a tight knot in her throat, and she knew that if she weren't careful, she might just cry.

Maybe, she told herself firmly, maybe it was

time she faced the sad truth about her and Justin Stone.

That he might have still loved her, but he didn't want a reconciliation.

He didn't want her back in his life.

NINE

Two days later Justin decided he was a fool.

Scowling, he tossed his pen onto his desk and leaned back in his swivel chair with a scrunch of well-worn leather. He was a fool to think he could stop wanting Morgan simply because he told himself he ought to, because he told himself it was the only sensible thing to do.

Because he couldn't.

He couldn't stop wanting her, couldn't stop thinking about wanting her.

Hell, he couldn't stop the feelings he had for her any more than he could stop the sun from rising each morning.

So maybe it was time he simply accepted the fact that he still wanted her, still needed her.

More than that, he still loved her.

Even though he knew it might very well destroy them both this time.

He dropped his gaze to the vinyl-encased pages of "Summer Heat" lying on his desk. Although he knew the opening by heart, he started to read it again.

> *Summer heat can do strange things to a man.*
>
> *I know because I met her in July, when the heat was at its peak. She was a cool kiss of springtime in a lilac dress. I stared at that frock, watching it whisper around her thighs as she moved, and I knew I would love her forever, knew it even before I knew her name.*

Justin traced the tip of his index finger across the line . . . *and I knew I would love her forever* . . . He smiled.

That was how it had been with Morgan.

He'd taken one look at her in her tennis whites standing in the kitchen of her father's house and he'd known, known it deep within his soul, that he'd love her until the day he died.

He squeezed his eyes closed for a moment.

But a reconciliation would never work, he told himself. No matter how much he still loved her. How could it when he'd loved her just as much six years before? Hell, love alone hadn't been enough to sustain their marriage then.

Common sense told him that he had to end this now, for both their sakes, before it went any further. After all, they'd gotten divorced—or tried to anyway—because they'd agreed it was for the best. It would be utter madness to try for a reconciliation.

Wouldn't it?

Sighing, he opened his eyes and raked his fingers through his hair.

Or did the madness come from thinking he could be satisfied with spending only one night in her arms?

Because he wasn't satisfied, and he couldn't forget how good it had felt making love with her again. He couldn't forget the silky smoothness of her skin and how the lush curves of her body meshed with his hard angles so perfectly.

Nor could he forget that making love with her was the only time he ever felt truly alive.

"Justin?"

His head jerked up at the sound of her husky drawl.

She stood in the doorway watching him, looking as heartstoppingly beautiful as ever. She wasn't wearing a lilac dress, though, or even tennis whites. She had on a burgundy sweater and skirt set, a body-hugging cashmere creation that sent a pang of longing straight through to his core.

His throat suddenly went dry, and his stomach muscles began to tighten.

"Ah, Morgan. Come in."

He pushed back his chair and stood. "I thought you were still at the center."

He walked around the desk.

She gave him a smile—one of those unerringly polite smiles whose warmth never quite makes it to the eyes—and walked toward him.

She'd changed since that night in the restaurant, he realized with a stab of regret. Changed in dozens of little ways. It was as if she'd stopped being Scarlett and had become Melanie: quiet, unobtrusive, unquestionably proper Melanie.

And he hated it.

Where Morgan had once called him "dahling" and would stroke his face or straighten his tie whenever the opportunity presented itself, she now did neither.

Where she'd once taken delight in teasing him, in pushing his self-control to its absolute breaking point with her husky southern drawl and a glimpse of her tanned thigh in a garter belt and silk stockings, she now just left him alone.

Just as he'd asked her to.

Just as common sense said it should be.

Hell, maybe he was worse than a fool.

"The center's closed now," she said quietly. "It's a quarter past five, or hadn't you noticed?"

"Ah, no."

He straightened the knot in his tie and glanced at his watch.

"I guess I got sort of wrapped up in my work," he said.

Or wrapped up in thinking about her.

She moved toward the desk. The floral fragrance of her perfume swirled around him, tantalizing him, beckoning him closer.

Intensifying his hunger.

He ached to reach out and pull her toward him, ached to hold her in his arms, to touch her silky skin one more time.

Ached to make the light shine in her sky-blue eyes again and hear that soft, tinkling laughter of hers.

"I see the programs finally arrived," she said, picking up one of the glossy-papered booklets from the stack on his desk. "How'd they turn out?"

She spoke so casually, as though she hadn't lain awake every night thinking about the same things he'd been.

As though she weren't haunted by the same images as he, or burning with the same unquenchable flame.

He closed his eyes and indulged in the memories.

Precious memories of her face flushed with passion, of the sensual pleasure of her hand gently touching him.

Erotic memories of the exquisite torture of her body squeezing his until his control shattered and he surrendered himself to her honeyed warmth.

Just thinking about it sent his heart pounding.

His eyes flew open, and he took a deep, steadying breath.

Morgan still stood next to him, quietly perusing the printed program. She seemed oblivious of his inner turmoil, though, oblivious of the desire for her that ran strong and hot through his veins.

Oblivious of him, period.

"You've done an excellent job," she said finally, lowering the program. She met his gaze. "You should be proud of yourself."

Oh, he'd done an excellent job all right, he thought bitterly.

An excellent job of losing her a second time.

"Thanks." The word came out a lot harsher than he'd intended.

She stared at him for a moment, then she smiled again. Warmer this time. More like her old self.

"Would you just look at you," she said softly. "Your hair's rumpled as if you just crawled out of bed and your tie's all askew. Why, you're looking so ragged around the edges, I swear you're beginning to sound that way too."

"But that's . . . not . . . why I'm sounding this way," he said huskily.

He reached for her hand, then pressed her warm palm against his cheek.

"It's because I'm standing so close to you," he said.

He wanted to kiss her, wanted to lose himself in her magic one more time.

She grinned. Her eyes began to sparkle and dance.

"Why, Justin Stone, I do believe you're flirting with me," she said.

"What if I am?" he asked, moving closer.

He grasped her chin with his other hand and tilted her face up to his.

"Would you really mind all that much if I were?"

Just one kiss, he told himself. What harm could there be in one little kiss?

"Hmm. I don't know," she said. "Flirting could give a girl ideas. It could make her think that—"

He leaned down and brushed his lips against hers, stopping her in mid-sentence.

Her mouth was as soft as he remembered. He moved the tip of his tongue against her lips and parted them gently . . . and she tasted just as sweet.

Their tongues eased together as though they'd never been apart, caressing, rubbing, beginning the slow, sensual dance he hoped their bodies would soon emulate.

He glided his hand around her waist, feeling the butter-soft cashmere of her sweater crinkle beneath his fingers, and pulled her closer. Her body fused with his, hip pressed against hip, thigh against thigh, breast against chest.

She felt so good in his arms. So right.

He began to massage her buttocks through the fabric of her skirt, pulling her closer against him until the pleasure of touching turned to the pain of not touching enough.

Until she groaned low in her throat and pushed him away.

He stared at her for a moment in confusion.

Her face was flushed, her eyes glittered with unchecked passion.

"The symposium," she said breathlessly. "It's time for your opening address. They must be waiting."

"So what?" Justin murmured, reaching for her again. "I'm sure Leonard—Cappy," he corrected himself with a grin, "can handle things fine without me."

He nuzzled the soft skin of her neck, teasing her with the tip of his tongue, the gentle rake of his teeth. He couldn't get enough of her.

Couldn't get enough of tasting her, of touching her.

"But you . . . you've worked so hard to make the symposium happen," she said.

"Forget the symposium," he whispered in her ear. "It's not important. Besides, Otto's lecturing on John Steinbeck tonight. I never much cared for Steinbeck. Did you?"

He ran the tip of his tongue along her earlobe and felt her shudder.

"Nooo," she murmured, making the word seem as if it had five syllables instead of just one. "Too much dust-bowl-evacuee business, not enough romance."

He laughed and hugged her to him.

"I'll give you all the romance you want," he promised. "We'll swing by that costume shop we talked about before. Remember? You were going to be the feisty serving wench while I was the lusty pirate. I'll carry you off to my bedchamber, where I'll slowly strip you of your clothes, then I'll—"

She pushed at his chest. "Justin, I . . . what are you saying to me? Exactly?"

He met her gaze, knowing he could get lost in her azure depths and not really caring if he did.

"I'm saying that I want to make love to you, Morgan," he said. "That I want you to make love to me. All night."

He paused, then added, "Every night."

Her heart pounding, her breath ragged, she stared at him for a moment.

She supposed she was making progress.

After all, a few short days before, Justin wouldn't have been able to admit that he wanted her, even though they'd both known otherwise.

Even though the evidence of his desire had been so clearly visible as to remove any possible doubt of its existence.

Now, without any encouragement on her part at all, he'd started to flirt with her, started to pursue her. Aggressively, in fact.

But all he'd really said was that he wanted to make love to her, she reminded herself.

He hadn't said that he loved her.

Or that he wanted her back in his life as his wife, his lifemate.

As much as she wanted to make love with him again, sex alone wasn't enough.

Not nearly enough.

"Now, Justin, stop teasing me," she said, pushing him back. "It's getting late. I think we'd better go."

"Forget the symposium," he said again, snagging her wrists. "I know I already have."

His gaze burned into her. Her heart began to flutter wildly in her chest.

"I want you to call me 'dahling,'" he said softly.

He pressed her palms to his chest. His body heat seeped through the thin fabric of his cotton shirt and washed over her, warming her from her head to her toes, making her knees feel weak and her insides start to melt.

"I want you to straighten my tie," he said, sliding his hands away from hers. "And touch my shirt."

He cupped her chin and stroked her face with his thumb, sending waves of liquid fire crashing around her last defenses. Her breath caught in her throat.

"Justin, I . . ."

She told herself to move away from him, to

put some distance between them before her control splintered into pieces, but she couldn't move.

She didn't want to move.

He kissed the edge of her jaw. The gentle brush of his lips burned her skin. The crisp, clean scent of his aftershave swirled around her, making her feel dizzy.

She closed her eyes and leaned closer.

"I was wrong to think we could fight this," he murmured, kissing her neck. "Wrong to think we should. Oh, Morgan, how I've missed you." His low voice was scarcely above a hoarse whisper.

He slid his hands onto her shoulders and began to massage her tense muscles. His fingertips scorched through the thick cashmere as if it were flimsy silk.

She moaned. She knew she was weakening.

"And you can't tell me you haven't missed me," he said. "Or that you haven't missed making love with me."

He slipped his tongue into her ear. Electric tingles shimmered down her spine, sending a sensual heat racing through her veins that set her nerve endings aflame.

"I . . . I wouldn't even try," she murmured.

How could she when she'd thought of nothing but him for days now? When she'd replayed every delicious moment of their night together in her mind, one slow frame at a time.

Just as she'd replayed every agonizing moment of their dinner in the restaurant the night after.

Regardless of how badly she wanted him just now—or how badly she knew he wanted her—it still didn't change the painful truth.

Justin didn't want a reconciliation.

Which was all that truly mattered.

She opened her eyes.

"Justin, I think we'd better—"

"Or poetry," he said, interrupting her. "Have you missed my making love to you with beautiful words, Morgan? Have you missed it as much as I have?"

His gray-green eyes, she noticed then, were smoldering with the same desire, the same all-consuming hunger that burned inside her.

" 'Oh! Yes, I will kiss thine eyes so fair,' " he said huskily, then he kissed her eyelids, first one and then the other. " 'And I will clasp thy form.' " He glided his hands around her waist and pulled her closer. " 'Serene is the breath of the balmy air, but I think, love, thou findest me' " —he took her hand and slid it down his abdomen to the growing bulge in his pants—" 'warm.' "

A shudder racked her body.

Percy Bysshe Shelley. Next to Byron, he was her favorite poet.

Especially the way Justin recited the verse.

She started to stroke him through the fabric of his trousers. He groaned low in his throat. Her heart began to pound harder.

"Justin . . ."

"Call me 'dahling,' " he said, kissing her neck again.

His kisses were harder, more frenzied. The power of his arousal pressed insistently against her hand. She felt as though she were being swept away by a force of nature that she was powerless to resist.

But this was madness, she told herself. Utter madness.

She shook her head, trying to clear the sensual fog that seemed to have enveloped her brain. Then she slipped out of his arms.

Taking a deep breath, she stepped back and met his smoke-tinged gaze.

"Justin . . . darling . . . I can't think of a lovelier way to spend the evening than making love with you."

He gave her that crooked smile of his.

The one that made her heart simply melt.

"Now, why do I sense that there's a 'but' in there somewhere?" he asked.

"But I can't," she went on.

"Why?"

"Lots of reasons," she murmured, dropping her gaze. "Mostly—" She looked up again. "Mostly because the offer I made you at the cocktail party has expired."

He took a step closer.

"You mean about our pretending to be Scarlett and Rhett for the night?"

His voice was as soft as a caress. It sent dozens of those tingles cascading down her spine again. She swallowed hard.

"But I thought I told you I didn't want you to be anyone but yourself?" he asked.

He reached for her again.

She stepped out of range, then moved to the other side of the desk.

"You did. But I'm afraid I can't spend just one night with you. I need more."

A lot more.

"Who says it has to be only for one night?"

She shook her head.

"But you want me," he said. "I know you do. Hell, ever since you got here, you've been reminding me of how good it used to be with you. Of how good it can still be. Dammit, why are you pushing me away now?"

"Because I . . . because I need more than sex from you, Justin."

She knew her voice sounded rough, knew she'd allowed more emotion to color her words than she'd wanted.

He stared at her for a moment longer. Then he sighed.

"Morgan, you know I care about you. I always have. I always will."

Care about you, he'd said. Not *love you*.

She felt her heart constrict.

"But I'm not convinced that we can pick up things where we left off six years ago," he said.

"We can't rush into a reconciliation. We need to take our time, think things through, see how we can fit into each other's lives. *If* we can fit into each other's lives."

He ran his fingers through his hair, making it look even more tousled than before.

"Hell, we rushed into marriage the last time and all it got us was a round-trip ticket to Costa Rica. I don't want to make the same mistake twice."

She smiled, or tried to anyway.

"But you were the one who said you couldn't wait," she reminded him. "Talking to me about fate and kismet and all. Saying you would simply curl up and die if I didn't marry you right then and there."

He grinned. "That's because I couldn't think straight when I was around you. I still can't."

He followed her around the desk.

"This is driving me crazy," he said. "All this arguing over something that's really very simple. We still feel things for each other. Can't we try to find some middle ground here? Somewhere between rushing into a marriage I don't think either one of us is ready for and shutting each other out of our lives forever?"

He caressed her chin again.

"If you care for me as much as I think you do," he murmured, "can't you try to meet me halfway on this?"

She held his gaze. "I don't think I can do

that," she said softly. "I want all of you . . . or none of you."

His jaw tightened. "So which one of us is being pigheaded now?"

She shrugged. "I spoke with Boyd Paul today," she said, changing the subject.

She walked around his chair, skimming her fingers along the smooth wood of his desk, wishing she were touching his bare skin instead.

"The judge in Los Angeles will grant the divorce as soon as he receives the signed papers," she went on. "Boyd Paul said he could have the preliminaries to us in a day or so."

"Morgan . . . it doesn't have to end this way."

She shrugged again. Then her fingers touched the coolness of vinyl, and she looked down.

She saw her father's familiar scrawl flowing across a blue-lined sheet of paper taken from a large notepad. It was the same kind of paper he'd always used to write his first drafts. Puzzled, she scanned the first line.

Summer heat can do strange things to a man.
She froze.

It can't be, she told herself. She must have misread the opening or maybe she was having a mild hallucination. It couldn't be "Summer Heat."

Then she slid through the vinyl-encased pages, quickly reading snatches of text.

But it was "Summer Heat."

Justin had a handwritten draft of her father's Pulitzer Prize–winning short story lying on top of his desk.

Even though she knew that couldn't be.

Even though she knew that was impossible.

She glanced up and met his gaze.

Was this supposed to be some kind of joke? she wondered in horror.

He smiled. "I wanted it to be a surprise."

It took her a moment to piece it all together.

His cryptic comments about the surprise of a "historic nature" he had planned for the workshop.

His hint about having found something remarkable in her father's papers.

The way he was smiling at her now.

"Oh my God," she whispered.

"E.J. had secured it to the back of his copy of *Tom Sawyer*," Justin explained, walking toward her. "Adam came across it when he was helping me catalogue the papers your aunt Libby donated to the university. At first I couldn't believe it. I mean, everyone know E.J. destroyed his first drafts."

"He said he couldn't bear to read them anymore," she said hoarsely.

He reached for her hand. "I once swore to you that if there were any way possible, I'd find one of your father's original manuscripts so you could read it. After the press conference this Friday, we can—"

She shook her head. "You can't do it."

"Excuse me?"

"You can't do the press conference. We have to cancel it, call it off. Something."

He frowned. "I can't call it off."

"Then I will."

He took a deep breath, then slowly released her hand.

"Morgan, I know how you feel about your father's work, but we can't keep this quiet. 'Summer Heat' is the literary find of the decade. Maybe even the century."

"Scam of the century, you mean," she said.

She stared at him for a moment in disbelief.

"Didn't you learn anything from all those years you spent studying Daddy?" she asked. "From reading his letters? From talking with Aunt Libby? He never saved his first drafts, Justin. Never. The manuscript's a fake."

TEN

Justin felt a sudden queasiness settle in the pit of his stomach.

"What are you talking about?" he demanded.

He snatched the vinyl-encased pages of the manuscript from her hands and did a quick review.

But everything was as he remembered. E.J.'s distinctive scrawl. The blue-lined pages he'd always used for writing his first drafts. Even the revisions scribbled in the margins.

Justin drew a sigh of relief. There was no question this was the genuine article, he thought. He was willing to stake his reputation on it.

Had staked his reputation on it, in fact.

He lowered the pages and met Morgan's worried gaze.

"It's your father's manuscript," he told her, more gently this time. "The original draft of

'Summer Heat.' I know. I authenticated it myself."

"Then you must have made a mistake."

Her jaw was set, her slender body rigid with tension. He couldn't recall a time when he'd seen her look more serious, more determined, about anything.

"It's a forgery," she said. "Granted, it's a very good forgery. So good that for a moment there I almost believed Daddy had written it."

He frowned. "So what makes you so sure he didn't?"

"Because I—" She took a deep breath. "Because I watched him destroy it, Justin." She met his gaze. "Because I watched Daddy throw 'Summer Heat' into the fire, one page at a time."

He stared at her, not sure what to say. He didn't doubt her sincerity, didn't doubt for a moment that she honestly believed what she was saying was the truth.

But he also didn't doubt the considerable evidence that said the manuscript was authentic.

She walked around the desk. "It happened on my tenth birthday," she said. "We were supposed to have this big party. Mama was there with her new husband, Sidney. Aunt Libby and Uncle Palmer were there too. And all my friends. Daddy spent most of the day in his office, though, smoking his pipe and drinking Jack Daniel's. It was chilly, the way February usually is in Mississippi, so we had a fire going in the fireplace."

She hugged her arms to herself as though she were still feeling the chill of that winter day.

"I don't know how it all started, really," she said. "All I remember is the yelling. Everybody running into the living room to find Daddy tossing pages from 'Summer Heat' into the fire while Catherine—that was daddy's third wife—screamed at him to stop. Mama tried to pretend nothing was wrong. She knew how Daddy could be sometimes, especially where his work was concerned. She herded everybody back into the dining room, but the party was ruined. We never did cut my birthday cake."

He felt something tighten deep inside him. "Why didn't you ever tell me about it?" he asked softly.

He wanted to pull her into his arms, wanted more than anything to kiss away the sadness from her eyes.

She shrugged. "It's not the way I like to remember Daddy. Besides, he made it up to me later, for the ruined birthday party, I mean. He took me to New Orleans that weekend, and we hung out in the French Quarter with these old jazz musicians. Guys who played with Louis Armstrong, people like that."

Her eyes were sparkling again. The lines of tension that had been etched across her forehead and around her mouth had faded.

"Daddy had 'em close the club and they jammed till dawn, putting on a concert for just us two. Mama 'bout had a fit when we got home, but it was worth it."

He grinned.

It was the kind of story about her father that Morgan loved to tell, rich with details of his boundless generosity and larger-than-life persona. Justin didn't blame her for wanting to forget that E.J. had a dark side to his genius.

A dark side that compelled him to destroy his work in fits of melancholy.

Justin's gaze dropped to the manuscript lying on top of his desk. He lifted a sheet and examined the still-wrinkled paper through the clear vinyl casing.

He sighed. He'd spent his entire professional career studying E. J. Tremayne, both the man and his work. Justin had built a reputation, one carefully researched paper at a time, for knowing more about E.J. than anyone else in the world.

So how could he have been so mistaken? Justin asked himself in self-recrimination. How could he possibly have allowed himself to be taken in by a forged manuscript?

"Maybe you only thought he destroyed it," he said, grasping at straws. "Maybe he destroyed some other manuscript. I mean, the handwriting, the paper—it all matches, Morgan."

She shook her head.

"Daddy destroyed 'Summer Heat,' Justin. That's why Catherine was so upset. Look, if you don't believe me, you can call Mama. She's spending the winter in Barcelona with friends."

She pulled an address book out of her purse.

"Catherine can confirm it, too, although it's not something she likes to talk about. She and Daddy split up a month after he burned the manuscript. And there's Aunt Libby. Call them. They'll all tell you the same thing I have."

"I believe you," he said, waving the address book away. "What I'm having a hard time accepting is why would someone go to all the trouble of forging a copy of 'Summer Heat.'"

He started to pace across his office, hoping the physical activity would help make some sense of the mystery.

"It's not as if the manuscript's for sale," he said. "So what could the forger possibly hope to gain by investing that much time and energy into creating a faked manuscript? And look where we found it—attached to the back of E.J.'s favorite book. It had apparently been stored in a box of other memorabilia for years. Hell, it might never have been found at all if your aunt Libby hadn't donated the papers to the university."

"But it is a forgery. I know it is."

"So who did it? Libby?" He shook his head. "She makes a helluva good pecan pie, but forging literary documents seems a little out of her league."

She was quiet for a moment. "I never thought Aunt Libby did it."

Her words stopped him cold. He turned to face her. "Meaning you think I did?" he asked.

"Of course not."

She grasped his arm. Her fingers burned through the fabric to his skin. Her gaze locked with his.

"I would never think that about you," she said. "Never. I just think you made a mistake when you authenticated it. That's all."

Her fingers dropped down to his hand and squeezed. The simple gesture sent fiery shivers racing down his spine.

It was amazing, he thought, feeling his body grow hard again. Morgan had just made an announcement that could quite possibly mean the end of his professional career. Yet, with just one stroke of her hand, she'd made him realize that he didn't care about his career or the scandal a forged literary document would likely bring to the university.

All he cared about, all he could think about, was her touching him.

And how much he wanted to touch her.

"What I think happened," she said, releasing his hand, "is that you so wanted the manuscript to be real, you didn't question it as thoroughly as you should have. Finding one of Daddy's first drafts, it was as much your dream as it was mine. I bet if you examined it again, you'd see right away that it was a forgery."

But that wasn't the point, he thought. He

should have seen that it was a forgery the first time.

She folded her arms and leaned against the edge of the desk to stare at him.

"Darling, you said Adam was the one who actually found it. Why was he examining the papers?"

"He's doing his master's on E.J.'s work. I needed some assistance in cataloguing, so Leonard suggested Adam. He brought the book to me as soon as he found it, though. It took me nearly half an hour to remove the manuscript from the back flap."

"I see."

She glanced down at the carpeting, then back at him.

"Adam just transferred to UCSB last year, didn't he?" she asked. "I remember Cappy saying something about his being brilliant but undisciplined."

Justin nodded. "Adam has been working on his master's full-time for nearly seven years now. UCSB's the third university he's attended, and E.J.'s the third or fourth area of study he's chosen."

She smiled. "He sounds like a professional student."

"Or something like that." He frowned. "But I doubt if he's responsible for this, Morgan. If Adam went to all the trouble of forging 'Summer Heat,' I'm sure he'd have wanted to take credit for the discovery, and he won't. Hell, he won't even discuss the possibility."

She nodded, then she met his gaze again.

"You know we have to tell Cappy about this, don't you?" she asked.

The queasy feeling in his stomach intensified. He nodded. "Yeah, I know."

The conversation, however, was not something he was particularly looking forward to. Probably because he knew the first question Leonard would ask would be why Justin hadn't realized the manuscript was a forgery before now.

Then he'd ask the same question that had been plaguing Justin for the past few minutes.

If "Summer Heat" was a forgery, who had done it?

More important, why?

On their way to the auditorium to find Cappy, Morgan chastised herself for breaking Justin's heart. For she knew that was what she'd done when she told him the copy of "Summer Heat" he'd discovered was a forgery. She'd broken his heart, shattered his dream into dust.

But what choice had she had?

She couldn't keep silent about the manuscript. Not when she knew he was about to destroy his career by announcing his discovery at the press conference on Friday. She'd had to tell him.

Even though she'd known that doing so would hurt him.

Even though she'd known that doing so might mean she would lose him forever.

Otto Koenig was well into his lecture on John Steinbeck when she and Justin slipped into the crowded auditorium.

Getting Cappy off the dais and back to Justin's office was easy.

Telling Cappy about the forgery was anything but.

"How the hell could something like this have happened?" he demanded once they'd explained their dilemma.

His bearded face was flushed and set in an angry scowl. He'd balled his hands into fists so tight that the veins in his neck were beginning to bulge.

"Good Lord, man! Didn't you check the damned manuscript out beforehand?"

Justin looked miserable, so miserable, Morgan began to ache for him.

"Of course I checked it," he said. "Very carefully, in fact. From the handwriting, the paper, the circumstances surrounding its discovery—I had no reason to doubt it was anything but an original draft of E.J.'s."

"But now you're just as certain that it's a forgery, is that what you're telling me?"

Justin shook his head. "No. That's not what I'm telling you."

He raked his fingers through his already tousled hair.

"What I said was that Morgan believes it's a forgery and, based on what she told me, I agree it could be possible. I'm going to reevaluate the manuscript, try to see where I made the mistake in authentication—*if* I made a mistake at all."

Still scowling, Cappy picked up the vinyl-encased pages of the manuscript from the desk and scanned them. A few seconds of tense silence followed, then his weathered features began to relax.

"It's a damn shame," he said softly. "The way E.J. always destroyed his work. Never could understand why . . ."

Cappy took a deep breath. He glanced at Justin again. "You're going to reexamine the other papers we received from Libby as well, aren't you? See if there're any more inconsistencies."

Justin nodded. "Absolutely. I don't know if we'll have a definite answer by Friday night, though. The wisest thing might be to cancel the press conference."

Cappy vetoed the suggestion.

"That will only make everyone wonder what's wrong," he said. "Better, I think, to keep this quiet and go ahead with the press conference as planned. Fortunately, the advance notice you released only made vague references to the topic to be discussed. We can either use the time to announce that we've uncovered an original manuscript of E.J.'s . . ."

Cappy carefully set the manuscript pages back on Justin's desk.

"Or that we've found the best damned literary forgery ever created."

Cappy glanced at Morgan. "I trust, my dear, that you'll help Justin in the reevaluation process. There are hundreds of papers to muddle through, and I think we'd all feel more comfortable if we kept this among ourselves just now."

"I'd be happy to help, Cappy," she murmured. "You know that."

Then she met Justin's suddenly unreadable gaze.

The only problem was, she was afraid Justin had had about all the help from her he wanted.

Less than forty-eight hours later, Morgan was ready to tell Cappy that they'd have to muddle through without her.

It was a simple matter of self-preservation, really. She was convinced she was going to go insane from having Justin sitting only inches away from her and not being able to touch him. She was so close that the scent of his aftershave swamped her, leaving her knees all shaky and her breathing ragged around the edges.

She told herself to think of something—any-thing—other than Justin, but she couldn't.

He was all she wanted to think about, all she could think about.

Each time he moved, she couldn't help but remember how good it felt to smooth her hands across his hard, muscled body.

Each time his gaze met hers and lingered for a moment, she couldn't help but fantasize about his lazy, bone-melting kisses and how he could send her senses positively reeling with a few whispered lines of Byron or Shelley in her ear and a touch of his hand.

If she'd still had her sense of humor—which she didn't—she might even have thought the situation funny.

After all, not too long ago she'd have given almost anything to be this close to Justin. To be able to spend hour after uninterrupted hour working with him in the close confines of his office and apartment.

Now she'd give almost anything not to.

"I've had about all of this I can take," Justin announced.

Morgan blinked at him. They were sharing his desk at the university. He sat in his leather swivel chair while she occupied the overstuffed armchair directly across from him.

For a moment she was certain he was reading her thoughts.

And for a moment her heart stopped.

"I need a break," he said, sliding the pages from "Summer Heat" aside. He rubbed his eyes. "How about you?"

"Ah, yes," she murmured, feeling herself blush. "I guess I do at that."

They'd been working on her father's papers for the better part of the day. Justin was leaving nothing to chance this time and was checking every possibility, no matter how remote.

He had sent out samples of the glue used to adhere the manuscript to the back flap of *Tom Sawyer* for testing and was having the handwriting on the manuscript analyzed by computer. He had a call into Aunt Libby—who was visiting friends in Tupelo, Mississippi, and wouldn't be back until late Thursday afternoon—to find out if anyone could have had access to E.J.'s copy of the Mark Twain classic before it was sent to the university.

Morgan, meanwhile, was supposed to review the other documents donated to the university for inconsistencies or any references to the original draft of "Summer Heat."

For the past thirty minutes, though—ever since Justin had removed his jacket to reveal the powder-blue cotton shirt that seemed tailor-made for his broad, sculpted chest—her ability to concentrate on the documents lying before her was in serious jeopardy.

In fact, her ability to breathe normally was in serious jeopardy.

He stood and slowly stretched, raising his hands over his head and flexing his shoulders. He moved with the deliberate sensuousness of some tightly muscled jungle cat or of a man who knows his every move was being watched by a woman he wants to impress.

He met her gaze and gave her a smile that warmed every part of her.

"I think there's still some coffee left," he said, referring to the pot they'd made hours before in his outer office. "Or would you prefer a soda instead?"

"Soda, I think," she said, feeling the blush in her cheeks being to deepen. "It's, ah, a little too warm in here for coffee."

She stood and followed him toward the door.

"Is it?" he asked innocently. "I hadn't noticed."

Grinning now, he opened the door, then stepped aside. Even so, her shoulder brushed his chest as she moved past him into the outer office. The casual contact sent liquid heat racing through her veins, just as a whiff of his aftershave threatened to overpower the last shreds of her rapidly vanishing willpower.

"Where's Sonia?" she asked breathlessly, glancing around the empty room, trying desperately to regain control of her out-of-control emotions.

"She has a class this afternoon," he said. "She won't be back until tomorrow morning. That's why she put up the Keep Out sign."

There was a hand-lettered sheet of paper affixed to the door of his outer office with a strip of transparent tape. The sign advised that all of Justin's classes had been canceled for the remainder of the week and that all student appointments would have to be rescheduled. NO ADMITTANCE—NO EXCEPTIONS had been added in big red letters.

They walked into the hallway and over to the vending machine. He dug into the pocket of his trousers and came out with several coins, which he deposited into the appropriate slot. He pressed the button for a diet soda. The clank of metal against metal sounded, then the can of soda landed in the tray. He reached for the soda, popped the tab, and handed her the can.

"Thanks," she said.

Their fingers touched. The icy coolness of the can of soda warred with the invigorating warmth of his hand, and the warmth won out.

Her gaze locked with his.

He smiled. "You're welcome," he murmured.

There was a husky edge to his voice. And an awareness of her as a woman shimmering in the smoky gray-green depths of his eyes. She knew, knew it with an absolute certainty, that he'd been feeling the same need for her that she'd been feeling for him all day.

Her breath caught in her throat. Her heart began to pound. And she waited.

Inexplicably, he turned back to the vending machine, dropped in more coins, and selected another diet soda.

Morgan leaned against the cool plaster wall,

not sure if her knees would support her weight any longer.

She took a long swallow of soda. Although it burned a fiery path down her parched throat, it did little to calm the rapid beating of her heart or the sudden flutter of thousands of butterfly wings in her stomach.

Voices reverberated down the long hallway. Laughter. Snatches of conversation. The sounds of students leaving one class to head to the next.

She glanced down the hall, then back at him. "I've, ah, been reading this letter to Daddy from his editor," she said, trying to refocus her attention on the project. "It's talking about publication dates for his next short story, that kind of thing. From the time frame, I'd say it was probably 'Summer Heat,' although the title of the story's not referenced."

He popped the tab on the can and took a long swallow of soda. "E.J. wrote 'Summer Heat' during his most prolific period. There were dozens of short stories and probably twice as many letters from editors."

"I know," she said. "But I keep hoping that I'll come across something about the manuscript in one of them."

Like maybe a reference to the fact that she was wrong and her father hadn't destroyed "Summer Heat" after all.

She'd never wanted anything as badly in her entire life as to give Justin back his lost dream.

"Chances are that's not going to happen," he said. "Not if the forger is as good as we think he is."

He set his can of soda on the top of the vending machine and placed his hands on her shoulders.

"But let's not talk about the damned manuscript right now," he said softly. "That's all we've talked about for the past two days. I'm tired of it, aren't you?"

The warmth of his touch seared through her silk blouse. A shudder slid down her spine.

"Oh?" she asked. "Then what do you want to talk about?"

"Who says we have to talk at all?"

He began to massage her muscles, gently at first, then harder, until she felt as if she were going to melt. She closed her eyes for a moment.

"You're so tense," he murmured in her ear. "Why don't you relax?"

"Relax?" she repeated. She opened her eyes and laughed. "How can I possibly relax when you're—"

He tipped her chin toward him and met her gaze.

"When I'm what?" he asked.

His voice was a husky whisper that sent waves of sensual heat spiraling around her.

"When I'm touching you?" he asked. "When I'm standing this close to you?"

Right on both counts, she thought.

"Is that how I make you feel, Morgan?" he asked, massaging her shoulders again. "Because it's how you make me feel."

He lowered his mouth toward hers.

"Justin!"

The familiar male voice rang out from somewhere down the hallway.

Justin cursed and stepped away from her. They both turned and watched as Adam Smiley hurried toward them.

"Glad I finally caught up with you," Adam said, sounding as out of breath as she felt. His pale face was lined with worry and his wiry red hair looked as though it hadn't been combed in a week.

"I've been calling you for the past two days," he said, "but Sonia won't put me through."

"Sorry," Justin said. "I've been busy."

Adam's gaze moved from Justin to Morgan. Adam nodded a greeting.

"I kind of figured you must be, since you canceled all your classes. I asked Leonard what was up, but he said he'd rather not say. Look," Adam said, frowning, "is there anything wrong? Something I should know about, I mean?"

Justin's gaze moved to her again. They'd agreed with Cappy not to say anything to Adam about the suspected forgery and had been dodging him for the past two days.

"No," Justin said. "Not a thing."

"Really?" Adam asked. "Because I've been

getting this horrible feeling that something's going on that I should know about. The press conference is only two days away, and you've canceled all your classes and gone into virtual seclusion. I mean, what am I supposed to think?"

Morgan searched for some bland reassurances, some meaningless words she could say that would put him off without making him wonder even harder about what they were up to.

"You see, Adam," she said, "Justin and I have been . . . that is, we've been trying to—"

"I guess you're about the only person around here who doesn't know about us," Justin said, interrupting her. He slid his hand around her waist and pulled her to his side. A comforting warmth coursed through her.

"What do you mean?" Adam asked.

"I mean that Morgan and I are married," Justin said. "That we haven't seen each other in a while and needed some time alone. I canceled the classes because we're trying to work out a reconciliation. Now, if you'll excuse us . . ."

Justin grabbed his soda off the vending machine with his other hand and headed back to his office with her in tow while Adam's jaw dropped to the floor.

Morgan tried to tell herself that Justin had said what he had only because he hadn't wanted Adam to know about the forged manuscript. She shouldn't read more into it than there actually was.

All the same, she couldn't help but feel a burst of renewed hope.

She couldn't help but think that maybe Justin still loved her.

And that maybe, just maybe, she still had a chance of winning him back.

ELEVEN

Justin and Morgan spent the next four hours working on E.J.'s papers, peering at yellowing documents and notes scribbled on the backs of envelopes and scraps of paper, then comparing them with the handwriting on the manuscript until Justin was convinced that eyestrain and unreleased sexual tension were both terminal conditions.

True, Morgan no longer flirted with him, but he was past the point where that was necessary. Merely sitting in the same room with her was enough to get his libido off and running.

When they got back to the apartment, he left her in the living room to review a few more documents while he retreated to the gym downstairs.

The workout didn't help, though.

He couldn't stop thinking about her, couldn't stop thinking about the sensual pleasure of having her tanned legs locked around his hips or the warmth of her breath against his neck as he held her while she slept.

He especially couldn't stop thinking about how, in a few short days, she'd be back in New Orleans and out of his life forever.

And that he had no one to blame for her leaving except himself.

After taking a long, cold shower—which did little to alleviate the need for her burning inside him—he returned to the apartment to find Morgan in the kitchen, trying her damnedest to look domestic.

There were at least half a dozen pots and bowls littering the counter and stovetop and she had smudges of flour on her cheeks. She had changed into jeans and a teal blue T-shirt. The aroma of baking chicken and boiling rice filled the air.

He grinned and leaned against the doorframe.

"I leave you alone for one hour and look what happens," he teased. "You're trying to cook. And after the fire department made you swear never to do it again."

Morgan's attempts at cooking had been a running joke in their marriage. Although she tried, she couldn't boil water without his having to triple the insurance policy limits. If it hadn't been for the weekly Care packages from her aunt Libby, they might have starved.

She grinned back at him. "Very funny," she

said, wiping her hands on a dishtowel. "You know as well as I do that the fire department had to come out only that once. And that was because you had lured me into the bedroom and the pot of red beans I was cooking ran dry."

He reached for her wrist and pulled her toward him. "Oh, is that how it happened?" he asked.

Her eyes started to sparkle.

"It is," she said. "And I'll have you know that I'm a pretty good cook. Why, I even took a couple of classes on the basics of Cajun cuisine just last summer."

"Good choice. Blackened anything was usually your specialty."

She hit him with the towel. He laughed and released her wrist.

"I keep telling you that I've changed," she said. "That I'm not the same spoiled—"

"You were never spoiled."

He brushed off the smudge of flour from her cheek. Her skin felt so soft. The muscles in his abdomen began to tighten.

"A little headstrong, maybe," he said. "And something of a free spirit, but what do you expect from E. J. Tremayne's daughter?"

Smiling, he tucked her hair back behind her ear and let his fingers linger on the curve of her earlobe.

"Mostly, though," he went on, feeling an ache deep inside him, "you reminded me of some beautifully decorated butterfly that fluttered around for a moment, brightening your life, then is gone forever."

"A butterfly? Oh, darling, what are you babbling about?"

He searched her gaze. He wasn't sure himself. There were so many things he wanted to say to her, so many things that needed to be said. If only he knew how to begin.

"Do you remember the day we met?" he asked softly.

A flush began to color her cheeks. She nodded.

"You'd walked into the kitchen looking for Aunt Libby," she said. "I'd just gotten back from the country club."

"You had on your tennis whites and you were drinking a glass of iced tea. You looked so tanned and fit and well cared for. I'd never seen anything more beautiful in my whole life."

"You weren't so bad yourself," she said huskily. "You had on those tight blue jeans and a cropped football jersey that showed off that body simply to die for."

Just the soft timbre of her voice was enough to make him grow hard. He closed his eyes for a moment and took a deep breath.

"That's when I fell in love with you," he said, stroking her cheek again. "Standing there in your father's kitchen. I'd never felt that way about anyone before or since. I wanted to do anything—be anything—to please you. I loved you so much that I thought I'd die when we got divorced in Costa Rica."

"So did I," she murmured. "I went to Europe with some friends afterward, but all I could think about was you. It took me six months to learn how to sleep through the night without having you lying next to me."

He sighed. It had taken him nearly a year.

And sometimes he still found himself holding his pillow and wishing it were she.

"But everything I did was wrong," he said. "It seemed the more I tried to hold on to you, the more I ended up pushing you away. You can't capture butterflies, Morgan. And you shouldn't try."

She slid her hand around his waist, sending a sensual warmth coursing through his veins. His mouth went dry.

"But I'm not some butterfly," she said. "I'm a woman. Flesh and bone."

She pressed herself against him, aligning her soft curves against his growing hardness.

"And you never had to do anything to keep me by your side," she murmured. "It was where I wanted to be. Where I was *meant* to be."

He stroked her hair. It felt like spun silk.

"No, you're not a butterfly," he agreed. "And you have . . . matured, I guess, is the best way to put it. I know I haven't told you this, but I'm really impressed with how hard you've worked over the past two days, helping me recatalogue and recheck everything. I couldn't have done it without you."

She pulled away to look up at him. "I was so afraid you'd be mad at me because I insisted the manuscript was a forgery."

"It wasn't your fault that I made a mistake. And I *did* make a mistake."

She frowned at him. "But the results of the analysis of the glue haven't come back yet. Or the computerized handwriting comparison. How can you be so sure it's a forgery?"

"I don't need them to tell me what I've already figured out," he said. "You saw E.J. destroy 'Summer Heat.' Besides, now that I've looked at the manuscript again, the penmanship seems a little too perfect, the revision process a little too predictable. What else can it be?"

"But . . ."

"No buts." He smiled. "You probably saved my career, Morgan. You've played Beowulf again, vanquished a few more Grendels, the way you do down at the center every day. Tricia told me about the role you played in getting that new legislation passed in Louisiana."

She grinned. "You know how I am when I set my mind to do something. And I guess I have 'matured,' as you say . . . although I still get an occasional yen for adventure." She raked her fingertips up his back.

"Oh?" he murmured. "What kind of adventure?"

"Hmm. Such as pirate fantasies or maybe playing out Scarlett and Rhett's big scene. The one lesson that Daddy said I should never forget is that you get only one chance at life."

His heart started to pound. "Like I had only one chance with you," he said softly.

"Two chances," she reminded him breathlessly.

She held his gaze for a moment.

"Somehow we got another one, thanks to that Costa Rican snafu," she said.

"Then let's not waste it," he said.

He lowered his head and kissed her. She sighed and molded herself to him, pressing closer and closer until he could feel the soft swell of her breasts through her T-shirt. Her mouth opened and he slid his tongue inside to meet the gentle thrust of hers. Her fingers wound through his hair.

He slid his hands down to her hips and pulled her against his arousal. He felt the shudder rack her body. He began to massage her buttocks through the stiff fabric of her jeans.

The rattle of a metal lid sounded, followed by the sizzle of a scorched pot. Then the unmistakable odor of burned rice filled the kitchen.

"My dinner!"

Morgan slid out of his arms and ran over to

try to salvage what remained of his saucepan and her rice.

"Now, this was not my fault," she said. "You distracted me again."

The doorbell rang.

"Explain it to the fire department," he teased. "That's probably them now."

She flung a pot holder at him and missed.

Still laughing, he walked into the living room and opened the door.

His apartment manager stood in the hall. Joe Dukakis, a slender man in his early fifties with thick black hair and bushy eyebrows, smiled and waved a large red, white, and blue envelope at Justin.

"I signed for this yesterday morning when the postman came. I've been meaning to come by sooner, but didn't have time. Hope it wasn't too important."

Justin's smile faded as his gaze dropped to the return address on the envelope. Boyd Paul Watkins, Attorney at Law. New Orleans, Louisiana.

Justin knew without having to open it what the envelope contained.

"Thanks," he muttered, feeling a knot form in the pit of his stomach.

Dukakis nodded, then turned and left. Justin quietly closed the door and flipped the deadbolt into place. He stared at the envelope again, knowing what he should do but not being able to do it.

"So was it the fire department?" she called out. The thud of her sneakers against linoleum followed.

Justin impulsively hid the envelope behind his back. "Ah, no. It was just Mr. Dukakis."

Morgan came out of the kitchen, drying her hands. She grinned. "What did he want?"

Justin met her gaze. Emotions tumbled through him. Pain. Regret. Longing.

Love.

He took a deep breath.

"Nothing," he said finally. "He just wanted to discuss some routine maintenance. I told him to catch me later."

She nodded and turned back to the kitchen.

Then he slid the envelope into the bookcase between two large volumes of southwestern art.

A few more days, he told himself. That's all he was asking for.

A few more days, then maybe he could let her go.

Morgan turned off the oven as Justin walked back into the kitchen.

"Well, the rice is gone but the chicken should be okay," she told him. "Fortunately, the salad didn't have to be heated. Otherwise—"

"It doesn't matter."

He slid his arms around her waist and pulled

her against him. "Let it all turn to charcoal. You're the only thing I want right now."

His lips nuzzled her neck, sending fiery shivers racing down her spine. His arousal was pressing into her lower back.

His hands moved up to touch her breasts. He began to caress her, alternating between gentle massages and painful tweaks of her nipples through the thin cotton of her shirt and lacy bra, touching her until a low moan came from deep in her throat.

Touching her until she arched her back and leaned against him for more.

His tongue slid around the edge of her ear. "Tell me something, Morgan," he whispered. "Are you in the mood for one of those adventures you talked about earlier? Like maybe Rhett and Scarlett?"

He nibbled her earlobe and thrust his hips against her buttocks. Liquid heat began to pool in her lower abdomen. Her heart started to pound.

"I—I think I could be persuaded," she said, amazed that she could still speak coherently.

She turned to face him. Passion burned in the gray-green depths of his eyes. It was a flame so hot, she could feel its heat sear into her soul.

He reached over and stroked her face with both hands, scorching her skin with the gentle brush of his thumbs.

"I should warn you, though," he murmured. "I don't have a winding staircase."

He kissed her forehead. His soft lips singed her flesh, making her knees feel weak. She closed her eyes as a tremor shook her.

"Nor one of those big canopied beds," he added, "like we had on our honeymoon."

He slowly slid his hands down her neck, caressing her with his fingertips, branding her with his touch. Then he dropped his hands lower, past her shoulders and over her now-sensitized breasts to her waist.

She opened her eyes and met his gaze. "I think we could improvise," she murmured. "Don't you?"

He gave her that crooked smile of his. Then he grasped her with both hands and lifted her up.

She wrapped her legs around his hips, wound her arms around his back, and clung to him. Cradling her bottom in his hands, he slowly kissed her, raking his tongue across her teeth and into her mouth to caress her tongue. His arousal pressed hard and strong against her groin. She started to move against him as the kiss deepened, wanting to feel him inside her.

He tore his mouth from hers with a groan. "I thought you wanted to make love in a bed," he said hoarsely. "Like normal people. Hell, if you keep doing that, we'll never make it past the dining room."

"I meant when we were very old," she protested. "Like when we're a hundred and one or so. But for now . . . for now I think the kitchen floor would be just fine."

He laughed. "The bedroom, Morgan. And in the bed. Just this once."

Then he slowly backed out of the kitchen to the dining room with her in his arms.

She loved the way his body felt, she thought, gliding her hands across his back. His muscles were so smooth and strong, his body so hard. His hair was still damp from the shower he'd taken after his workout, and he smelled of talcum powder and soap.

She tugged at his sweatshirt, wanting to touch his bare skin as he carried her down the hall. She slid her hands along his back, feeling the muscles undulate under her fingers, feeling the shudder slide down his spine as she kissed his neck. She moved again, pressing herself closer, rubbing herself against his growing hardness.

"But it's a long way to the bedroom, darling," she teased.

He groaned and kicked open the bedroom door. "I thought you wanted to be Scarlett tonight. You're acting more like the lusty pirate."

He loosened her grip on his hips and gently dropped her onto the middle of the bed.

She giggled. "Sorry. Wrong fantasy."

"Not that I'm complaining, mind you," he said, and gave her a wolfish grin. "I think a little role reversal's fine."

He dove after her and kissed her again. His

warm tongue sought out hers, turning the giggle about to erupt into a low, deep moan. His hands caressed her body, moving from her shoulders to her thighs in carefully measured strokes, over and over and over again until all she could do was gasp and hold him close. Then his hand slid between her legs to touch her through her blue jeans.

He pressed the palm of his hand against her, slowly at first, then using a harder rhythm that made her blood turn to liquid fire and soft moans escape from her throat. She squirmed as the coarse denim of her jeans rubbed against her panties, sending waves of pleasure crashing over her. She whispered his name and arched her body toward him.

He raised his head to meet her gaze. He brushed back her hair from her forehead.

"I want this to last," he whispered hoarsely. "I want us to remember this night for the rest of our lives."

She stared into his passion-flecked eyes. "Like . . . like when we're down at the rest home?" she asked breathlessly. "Inspiring that whole generation of lovers we talked about? Is that what you mean?"

"Exactly."

He slid his hand between her legs again.

But this felt too good, she thought, squeezing her eyes closed as he rubbed his palm across her. It couldn't possibly last much longer. She felt as if she were going to splinter into pieces any second now.

He tugged the T-shirt out of her jeans, then pressed his lips against her heated skin. A shudder rippled through her. He ran the tip of his tongue over the same spot, sending fiery tremors tumbling down her spine.

"Your skin feels like silk," he murmured. "So soft."

He eased the T-shirt up her body to expose her bra. He traced his fingers over the lacy cotton, slipping a finger inside to stroke her. White-hot shivers shimmered down the length of her, engulfing her body in a heat so hot, she wasn't sure she could survive its power.

"Oh, Justin." She moaned softly.

She opened her eyes and met his fevered gaze. She wanted to tell him that she loved him, wanted to tell him a thousand different things about the way he made her feel, but it was difficult to articulate words just then. So she reached for his hands and tried to pull him closer, wanting to show him how she felt, but he stayed just tantalizingly out of her reach.

He lowered his head to her breasts. His tongue raked across the flimsy fabric of her bra, wetting her hardened nipples, teasing her, tormenting her, taking her to heights of pleasure she'd never known existed. First with one breast, then with the other, he took her higher and higher until she couldn't stand the pleasure any longer.

She struggled into a sitting position and yanked the T-shirt over her head. Her fingers shook as she reached behind her and unclasped her bra.

He stilled her movements and kissed her shoulders, making her skin sizzle from the brush of his tongue and the tender caress of his lips. He slowly slid the lacy straps down her arms, then eased her breasts out of the cups so he could touch her.

He gently caressed her, as though he were afraid that rough handling might somehow break her, as though he were trying to burn the memory of touching her this way into his very soul. He rubbed the tips of his fingers over her nipples, now tightened into two buds, and kissed the bony ridge between her breasts.

He trailed a path of fire-laced kisses down her abdomen to the waistband of her blue jeans. His hand eased between her legs again and rubbed her, bringing her closer and closer to an internal meltdown.

"You're so hot," he murmured. "You feel like you're on fire."

"Simply . . . burning up," she agreed.

And he was the reason why.

His hands reached for the metal snap of her jeans. He undid it, then slid the zipper down.

He pulled away for a moment and tugged on

her jeans. She raised her hips so he could pull the jeans down her thighs and off her legs, along with her sneakers. He eased her panties off with the same fluid motion.

"Why don't I cool you down a bit?" he asked softly.

He pressed his lips against her inner thigh, parting her legs with a gentle push of his hands, sending streaks of red-hot fire shooting through her body. She gasped as his lips moved closer and closer to the place where she wanted him to touch her most of all.

Cool her down, he'd said? She shook her head in disbelief. It seemed to her that he was trying to incinerate her.

His lips brushed against her, setting her nerve endings aflame, then his warm tongue slowly raked across her sex. She gasped and arched her body toward his mouth. His tongue slid over her, wetting her, teasing her, loving her. Again. And again. Until she thought she'd go mad from the pleasure of his touch. Then his tongue moved past the folds of her flesh to lick her nub of throbbing desire.

Yes! her brain screamed. *Oh, God, yes.*

She moaned his name and tried to twist away from the sensual onslaught but couldn't seem to make her body respond to her brain's commands.

She reached for him but got only his hands. He interlocked their fingers and squeezed. Pressing her hands to the bed, he continued to pleasure her as only he could. His tongue slowly slid inside her, probing her wetness, then slowly pulled back. Just in and out. Over and over again.

No, she thought, feeling the fireburst build inside her. This wasn't the way she wanted it to happen. She needed to hold him, needed to feel his arms wrapped around her. But she couldn't help herself. She was careening through space, tumbling with the power of the climax that he'd unleashed inside her.

She cried out as the release overtook her. She wasn't sure what she said, knew only that she'd screamed something as the mad rush of sensations swamped her. Afterward, as she lay there trembling, tears welled in her eyes at how beautiful he'd made her feel. Not with words, not with poetry written by the masters. Only with his touch.

He moved alongside her and pulled her into his arms. He held her until her heart stopped pounding and her erratic breathing slowed, held her until she realized that his skin felt as feverish as hers had felt moments before. She shifted slightly and heard him draw in his breath. His arousal still pressed firm and hard against her abdomen.

He'd done this for her, she thought with amazement. All for her. He'd shoved his own needs aside to bring her to a soul-shuddering release, then he'd held her tightly in his arms afterward.

She looked into his eyes, searching his gaze for an explanation. She saw passion there. And desire. But more.

So much more that her heart began to constrict.

She struggled with his sweatshirt, helping him pull it off and toss it aside. She smoothed her hands across his bare chest and reached for the elasticized band of his sweatpants. He pulled away for a moment and jerked his pants off, then tossed them to the floor.

She stroked him, feeling the power and strength of his erection against her palm. She wanted to return the pleasure he'd shown her, wanted to make him feel as wonderful as he'd made her feel.

She wanted especially to show him with her touch just how much she loved him.

"I . . . can't . . . last much longer," he said with a groan. His fingertips pressed into her shoulders.

She leaned back on the bed and pulled him toward her. "Then let go," she murmured.

She moved her legs around his waist, tilted her hips toward him, urging him inside her.

He hesitated a moment. His gaze locked with hers. Emotions warred across his face. Her heart felt as though it would simply burst.

"I love you, Morgan," he murmured hoarsely. He slowly thrust into her, guiding her legs around his hips and his hands under her buttocks to pull her to him.

"I love you," she echoed, closing her eyes. She hugged him closer, squeezing him with her legs, milking him with the walls of her body until the power of his release shook him and he cried out her name.

"I love you," he whispered again.

TWELVE

Justin awoke shortly after dawn. He lay in bed for a long while, just holding Morgan in his arms and listening to her slow, rhythmic breathing. Even if he'd tried, he couldn't think of a better way to spend eternity than lying there, feeling her warm body nestled against his.

He sighed and gently stroked her hair.

But he wasn't sure if they could have an eternity together. Or anything beyond a few more days. She'd made it clear that she wanted a reconciliation or nothing at all.

And he wasn't sure if he could make a commitment again, even though he loved her.

Even though he knew she still loved him.

Even though he knew the problems that had once plagued their marriage—his insecurity over having a rich wife and his fear she would regret marrying a penniless post-grad student; her uncertainty over what she wanted to do with her life and her unquenchable passion for all-night parties—were now little more than ancient history.

Even though he knew their lives now meshed perfectly.

He was still afraid to commit, still afraid he would only get hurt again.

She began to stir. She slowly stretched, murmuring deep in her throat, then snuggled closer.

"Justin?"

Her voice was a low, throaty drawl that sent his pulse racing.

"Good morning," he said huskily, stroking her hair again.

Her hand skimmed lightly over his abdomen. "Good morning, darling."

Her touch was like fire, he thought with amazement. Liquid heat began to race through his veins. His body tightened, grew hard.

She raised her head to meet his gaze. She was so beautiful in the mornings, he thought, feeling a pang of longing that cut straight to his core. Her hair was mussed and tumbling around her face, and her eyes had a hazy, dreamlike quality that simply took his breath away.

His hand slid down her face to cup her chin. He leaned over and kissed her softly on the lips. The flames inside him fanned even hotter.

"What time is it?" she asked, sliding her hand down his body to touch him.

"Almost seven," he murmured.

He closed his eyes as her fingers wrapped around the length of him, gently massaging him into full arousal.

"The, ah, alarm should go off any second now," he added.

Her lips brushed his chest, scorching his skin. His erection pressed hard and strong against her palm.

"Couldn't we bury the clock in the clothes hamper or something?" she asked. "The way we used to?"

He chuckled. "And unplug the phone? So we can spend half the day in bed?"

"Mm-hmm. Unless you have any better ideas, darling."

He didn't.

He told himself that he was only prolonging the inevitable. He told himself that eventually he'd have to tell her about the divorce papers he'd hidden in the bookcase.

Eventually he'd have to decide whether to agree to a reconciliation . . .

Or just let her go.

The alarm sounded.

He reached for her mouth. Their tongues came together in a frenzy of need, rubbing, caressing, sucking in wild abandon. His hand cupped her breast. He began to stroke her, feeling her nipple begin to harden against his fingers.

Without breaking the kiss, he leaned over with his other hand and yanked the cord to the clock-radio out of the wall, permanently silencing the alarm. Then he pulled her on top of him.

Who was he trying to kid? he asked himself. He could never give her up.

Never.

She knew they should have unplugged the phone, Morgan thought, jerking awake a few hours later when it began to ring.

And ring.

And ring.

Justin's hands tightened on her waist as she leaned over to grab the receiver.

"Hello," she murmured.

"Morgan? It's Leonard Capshaw. I was about to give up on you guys."

Justin's lips pressed against her shoulder. "Hang up," he murmured.

He traced the tip of his tongue along her skin, sending fiery shivers cascading down her spine.

"Oh, hi, Cappy," she said, ignoring Justin— or trying to anyway.

"I thought you two were going to be working on E.J.'s papers down here at the university," Cappy said. "Did you change your mind?"

She glanced at the clock-radio. It still read seven, which she knew was incorrect. She picked up Justin's wrist and glanced at his watch. Ten-fifteen.

"Ah, no," she said. "We're still planning to

come down there. We just sort of . . . well, we fell back asleep, I guess."

"Liar," Justin said softly.

His hand eased around her breast, rubbing his finger across the sensitive skin of her areola. Her nipples began to harden. Fluid heat started to swirl in her loins.

"Good," Cappy said. "Because I think I solved our little mystery about the manuscript. I placed a call to a friend of mine at the University of Nevada, where Adam used to attend classes before transferring to UCSB. It seems 'Summer Heat' isn't the first forged manuscript he's uncovered."

"Really?"

"Tell him we'll call him back," Justin whispered.

He pulled her toward him. The satiny warmth of his shaft pressed against her buttocks. He gently rubbed himself against her. A shudder racked her body.

She struggled into a sitting position.

"What happened?" she asked huskily, pushing Justin away.

He only grinned at her and propped his head up with his elbow.

"His previous specialty of study was Ernest Hemingway," Cappy said. "He was helping inventory some papers and apparently uncovered a handwritten letter by Hemingway, which he turned over to the department chair. Adam declined to share credit for the discovery, though."

"But that's almost exactly what happened this time," she said.

"I know," Cappy said. "Fortunately, they discovered the forgery before any announcements were made. They suspected Adam was responsible but couldn't prove anything. He transferred and the subject was dropped."

"So what do you want to do, Cappy?"

"Confront him with what we suspect. See what he has to say for himself."

She heard him strike a match and light his pipe.

"When do you think you and Justin can meet me down here?" Cappy asked.

She glanced at Justin. His gray-green gaze burned into her, warming her all over. His fingers skimmed along the skin of her back.

"An hour," she said, feeling slightly out of breath. "Maybe a little longer."

"Good enough," Cappy said, and rang off.

She hung up the receiver. "Darling, Cappy knows Adam forged the manuscript. It seems that he—"

"Shh," he murmured, and pulled her closer. "It can wait."

Then his lips claimed hers in a passionate kiss.

He was right, she thought with a moan as she slid into his embrace.

Everything—the whole damn world, in fact—could wait just a little longer.

Morgan's estimate was off by about an hour or so. They didn't get to the university until half past twelve. By then, Cappy was no longer in his office and most of the faculty members were at lunch.

Rather than waste any more time, she suggested that Justin go look for Cappy while she waited in the office for them to return. Justin seemed hesitant to leave her—after all, she was wearing her brown leather miniskirt and his gaze hadn't strayed far from her legs since she'd gotten dressed—but he finally agreed.

When ten minutes passed and still no Cappy —or Justin, for that matter—Morgan wandered back into the outer office, where Adam's desk was located.

Everything seemed neat and orderly, without so much as a paper clip out of place. She sat down on the charcoal-colored swivel chair behind his desk and rested her chin on her open palms.

She sighed. There seemed little doubt that Adam was responsible for the forged manuscript. The only thing she couldn't figure out was why he'd done it.

It seemed to her that he didn't stand to gain anything from the forgery—no monetary compensation, no fame, no boost to his academic career. Nothing at all except maybe the knowledge that he had tricked the experts.

Then the proverbial light bulb flashed above her head.

Maybe that was it, she thought, straightening. Maybe Adam had done it only to prove he could outsmart the so-called experts. According to Justin, Adam had been working on his M.A. full-time now for seven years. Maybe he was jealous of Justin. Maybe forging literary documents was Adam's way of evening the score, of proving that he was smarter than everyone else.

Her fingers glided over the scarred wood of his desk. It must have taken him weeks of painstaking work to complete the forgery, though, weeks to get the handwriting right. A project like recreating "Summer Heat" would surely require many dry runs before he attempted to do the actual manuscript. Maybe, she thought, feeling her heart begin to pound, there were even a few samples of his handiwork still lying around to substantiate their theories.

Before she could talk herself out of it, she opened the top drawer and rifled through its contents but found only pads of paper and ball-point pens. Then she pulled out one of the larger drawers. It held nothing but manila file folders containing Cappy's class schedules and other administrative documents. Frowning, she closed the drawer and reached for the next. Nothing.

Refusing to give up, she turned to a small

metal filing cabinet on the floor next to the desk. She tried to open it, but the release wouldn't give. Adam had locked the cabinet. She slowly smiled.

She reached for a paper clip, unfolded it, and started picking the lock. The cabinet was similar in design to one her father used to have. Because he kept losing the key—or maybe because it was just more fun that way—he'd taught Morgan how to pick its lock before her eighth birthday.

She'd almost gotten the cabinet open when she heard footsteps slowing at the hallway door.

"You're wasting your time, Morgan," Adam said. "I never keep any of my rough drafts on campus."

His calm, emotionless voice sent a chill racing down her spine.

"Adam, you startled me," she said, trying to sound as carefree as she possibly could. "I was just looking for a piece of paper so I could leave Cappy a note. I couldn't find any on your desk and thought—"

She looked up to meet his gaze and stopped.

A clever excuse and a winning smile wouldn't help her this time, she thought, feeling an icy fist wrap around her heart.

Adam Smiley looked as though he were past listening to anything she had to say.

What's more, he was pointing a gun straight at her.

Justin knew something was wrong when he and Leonard arrived back at Leonard's office. The outer office door was closed and Justin distinctly remembered having left it open.

He exchanged a worried glance with Leonard, then slowly opened the door. Justin could hear voices coming from Leonard's office a few feet away. Justin recognized Adam's voice, hard and angry.

Then Morgan's.

Fear coiled in Justin's stomach. He muttered a curse.

"I'll call security," Leonard said, quietly taking charge. He moved to the phone at Adam's desk and punched in a series of numbers.

"Morgan?" Justin called out.

Knowing he should wait until security got there but not being able to control himself, he stormed across the room and pushed open the door to Leonard's office.

Morgan stood next to the desk, looking so terrified that Justin wanted to cry out in pain. Adam held a small handgun in his right hand. Its nose was pointed dead even with Morgan's midsection.

"Don't come any farther," Adam said in a wavery voice. The gun started to wobble. "I don't want to shoot her, but I will if I have to."

Justin went rigid. "So help me, Adam, if you harm even one hair on her head . . ."

"Darling, I'm all right," she said quickly.

Her gaze locked with his. He could see the terror in her sky-blue eyes, the fear. But it was fear more for his safety than her own, he realized with a start.

"I'm okay," she told him. "Really. Adam and I are just talking. There's nothing to worry about."

"Let her go, Adam," Justin said. He took a step forward.

Adam shook his head. "I can't do that." Then he waved the gun at Justin. "I thought I told you not to come any closer, Justin. Dear God, are you trying to make me kill somebody?"

Justin stopped. He clenched his hands into fists.

"Adam, don't be a complete fool," Leonard said from the doorway. "Put down the gun. Let's talk this through like reasonable men."

Adam only laughed.

"I'm sure we can work something out," Leonard went on, coming to stand alongside Justin. "So far you haven't hurt anyone. We could try to keep this quiet. The university doesn't want a scandal any more than I imagine you do."

"A scandal?" Adam's face twisted into a bitter smile. "It's a little late to worry about that, don't you think? Besides, no one would have ever known about it at all if Morgan had kept her nose out of it."

Adam waved the gun at Morgan again. Justin's blood ran cold. This was like having a nightmare, he thought. The kind where you're unable to move, the kind where you can only stand there and watch as the monster moves slowly closer.

Morgan stood less than ten feet away from him, but she might have been miles away for all the help he was to her. But as long as Adam pointed a gun at her, there was nothing Justin could do except watch.

And pray.

"Did you really think I wouldn't know what you were up to, Justin?" Adam asked. "Outside your office yesterday afternoon when you told me that you and Morgan were married, I mean? Just how stupid do you think I am?"

Very stupid, Justin thought.

And very dangerous.

Which made for a lethal combination.

"But Morgan and I are married," Justin said quietly. "We met while I was working on my doctoral thesis on E.J. We got divorced—or thought we did anyway—six years ago in Costa Rica. There was a paperwork snafu. The divorce didn't take. And we're working on a reconciliation, just as I told you."

A look of surprise crossed Leonard's weathered face. His gaze shot from Justin to Morgan.

"Well, I'll be damned," Leonard muttered under his breath.

Adam just shook his head in confusion. "I don't—"

"Even if I hadn't said anything about 'Summer Heat' being a forgery," Morgan said, "other people would have known it was one."

She was talking in soothing tones, the way Justin imagined she did with a hard-to-reach child down at the center.

"Aunt Libby would have known," she went on. "And Mama. Catherine too. And there were over twenty kids at my birthday party. We all watched Daddy burn 'Summer Heat,' Adam. People would have known the manuscript was a forgery, no matter what I said or did."

"She's right, Adam," Justin said. "And I'd have figured it out eventually."

"Stop it," Adam said. "I don't believe you."

"Adam, I spoke with Jim Popejoy over at the University of Nevada," Leonard said, taking a step closer. "He told me about the Hemingway letter. We'd have found out about 'Summer Heat.' Just as Morgan said."

Adam flushed an even deeper crimson than his hair.

"Popejoy could never prove anything, Leonard," he said. "He may have suspected, but he couldn't prove a damn thing."

Justin took a slow step forward, his gaze never

wavering from Morgan's face. All he'd need was one brief distraction, then he'd tackle Adam, wrestle the gun away.

"Why, Adam?" Leonard asked, shaking his head. "Why all the forgeries? You could have had a brilliant career ahead of you if you'd just applied yourself. Why in the name of God did you throw it all away?"

"Why?" Adam's voice was angry. "Because I'm tired of seeing people with less talent than I have make it while the university closes its ranks against me."

Adam turned toward Justin. "You thought 'Summer Heat' was the real thing, didn't you, *Professor* Stone? You told me it was the literary find of the decade, didn't you? And yet you call yourself an expert on E. J. Tremayne. Hell, you were even married to his daughter and you couldn't see that the manuscript was a forgery."

The gun started to wobble again. Justin took a step closer. Morgan shook her head.

"So you fooled me, Adam," Justin said quietly. "I admit it. You fooled us all."

"You can't blame the university for your problems," Leonard said, trying to force Adam back on track. "You kept changing your area of study, that's why it's taken you so long to graduate. You could have gotten your master's five years ago if you'd only stuck with a topic."

Adam shook his head. "There was always

someone trying to stop me. They were jealous of me, still are."

Adam's eyes started to glitter dangerously. "I forged my first literary document four years ago at UCLA just to prove that I could do it. I was doing my master's on the works of Edgar Allan Poe. All the professors there were so damned pompous. No one would take me seriously when I proposed a new theory about the symbolism of Poe's 'The Raven.' "

Adam waved his hand in the air. The gun dropped lower. Justin held his breath.

"So I forged a letter from Poe to a friend of his," Adam went on. "I made sure it had a reference to my theory. It wasn't a very good forgery —even a first-year lit student could have recognized it for what it was. But did those pompous jackasses realize it was a fake? No, they just rejoiced over their new 'discovery.' "

Justin heard the sounds of footsteps, of quiet movement, at the office door behind him. He knew without turning around that it was the security officers Leonard had summoned. Justin could only hope that they wouldn't try to force Adam into some kind of showdown.

Not while Morgan was still in the line of fire.

The gun started to wobble again.

"No one understands what it's like trying to earn your M.A. when the whole system's against you," Adam said. The gun swung away from Morgan. "No one understands all the agony—"

Everything happened at once. Justin rushed forward. Morgan's hand shot out, hitting Adam's wrist. The gun flew out of his grip and landed on the floor. Adam dove for it, but Leonard reached it first and kicked the gun out of the way. Justin grabbed Morgan's arm and pulled her to safety as security men stormed into the room.

"It wasn't loaded," Adam screamed as security officers wrestled him to the floor. "I swear to you, the gun wasn't even loaded."

It took nearly an hour for Justin's heart rate to return to normal.

Finding out that the gun hadn't been loaded had done damn little to lessen his anxiety level. The fact that Adam had been desperate enough to bring a gun to campus in the first place—desperate enough, in fact, to hold Morgan hostage—would likely give Justin nightmares for weeks to come.

By the time the police escorted Adam away, the press were swarming outside Leonard's office, clamoring for interviews. Leonard suggested, and Justin agreed, that they cancel the press conference scheduled for Friday and hold one instead at five that evening.

After advising the reporters of the change in plans, Leonard then went to confer with the administration officials on how they wished to handle the incident, while Justin and Morgan returned to his office to prepare a brief statement.

The only problem was that Justin couldn't keep his mind on the statement they were supposed to be writing.

Not with Morgan sitting on his desk just inches away from him, that is.

Not with her tight leather miniskirt hugging her tanned thighs.

Not when all he could think about—all he wanted to think about—was how warm and smooth her skin would feel beneath his bare hands.

And how much he loved her.

"You realize, don't you," he said, leaning back in his chair with a scrunch of well-worn leather, "that Leonard's calling you the woman of the hour?"

He traced his index finger down her leg to the curve of her ankle.

"What with the way you disarmed Adam with that karate chop of yours," he murmured. "I don't think Scarlett O'Hara could have done better defending Tara from Yankee invaders. Although if you ever do anything like that again, I'll probably die of heart failure."

She laughed and leaned over to stroke his cheek. Shivers tumbled down his spine, warming him to the depths of his soul.

"And what about you?" she asked in that low,

throaty drawl of hers that sent his heart pounding again.

"I mean, you looked as though you wanted to tear Adam limb from limb," she went on. "And when you came dashing into the office to rescue me with your eyes blazing fire and all, I swear you looked for all the world like some centuries-old pirate boarding a frigate. It was so romantic."

Her gaze locked with his. "And so terrifying," she added softly. "All I could see was Adam firing that gun at you. I've never been so scared in my entire life."

Nor had he.

He took a deep breath and tried to block the memories, tried to concentrate instead on the floral scent of her perfume, on the feel of her warm palm against his cheek.

"It's like I keep telling you, I guess," he said. "You bring out the pirate in me."

He slid his hands around her waist and pulled her into his lap. Lips met lips, tongue caressed tongue in a slow, deep kiss that he never wanted to end.

Sometime later he pulled back to meet her passion-flecked gaze. Her face was flushed and her breathing was as erratic as his.

"I, ah, guess we really should be writing our statements," he said. "The press conference is only an hour away."

"We have plenty of time," she said, winding

her arms around his neck. "Besides, Cappy said we should keep it brief, remember?"

He smiled. "Good point."

His lips brushed against hers again. She sighed and leaned closer. A knock rapped on the door.

They both pulled away as Sonia stuck her head into the room.

"Sorry to interrupt," she said, grinning, "but there's a guy out here who swears he's got a four o'clock appointment with you two."

Justin frowned. "Tell him he's mistaken."

It had to be a mistake. His calendar had been cleared through Friday and all appointments rescheduled. Besides, he didn't recall ever having anything set for this afternoon anyway.

"Maybe it's a reporter," Morgan suggested, sliding out of his lap. She tugged at her tight leather skirt, pulling it back into place.

"Unh-unh," Sonia said. "He says he's your attorney. A Boyd Paul somebody or other."

Morgan's smile vanished. "Boyd Paul?" she repeated hoarsely.

"Right here in the flesh, honey," boomed a hearty baritone through the open doorway.

Justin's stomach tightened into a knot as a large, dark-haired man wearing a cowboy hat barreled his way into the office seconds later. The man slid a custom-made black leather briefcase onto the middle of the desk.

Boyd Paul Watkins—for there was little doubt

in Justin's mind that was who the man was—glanced from Morgan to Justin, then started to chuckle.

"Now, what's with the long faces? I know I'm a little late, but traffic out of LAX was something fierce."

THIRTEEN

"Late?"

A wave of panic flashed through Morgan. She squeezed her hands into fists to keep them from shaking.

"What are you talking about, Boyd Paul?" she asked. "You're not late. We weren't expecting you at all."

Boyd Paul laughed and snapped open the lid of his briefcase.

"Now, darlin', I know I had my secretary mail you a letter letting you know I'd be by here around four this afternoon with the divorce papers. She sent it out next day delivery on—now, let me see."

Boyd Paul pushed back the brim of his cowboy hat and scratched his head.

"It was Monday, I believe," he said. "Along with a summary of the papers I'd be bringing for you to sign. You should have gotten it by Tuesday afternoon at the latest. Maybe it just slipped your mind."

"But I never got any letter."

She could never have forgotten something like Boyd Paul flying out from New Orleans with the divorce papers, regardless of how hectic the last few days had been.

Her gaze flew toward Justin. He'd picked up a ball-point pen from his desk and was rubbing his thumb along its edge. A frown creased his forehead.

Sonia's grin slid off her face. She looked as disappointed as Morgan felt herself.

"I'll, ah, be outside if you guys need me for anything," Sonia said. Then she left the room and quietly closed the door behind her.

Boyd Paul turned to Justin and extended his hand. "You must be Professor Stone. I'm Boyd Paul Watkins. It's a pleasure to meet you."

The two men shook hands and began making small talk about the deplorable traffic conditions in southern California or something equally as mundane.

Morgan started pacing around the office. This couldn't be happening, her brain screamed. Not now. Not when they'd come so far.

All they needed was a little more time, she thought, wrapping her arms around herself. They were so close to working things out, so close to finding that happy ending she felt they both deserved. The night before, Justin had told her he loved her. A few more days, and she knew she could convince him that they belonged together.

A few more days, and there would have been no need for Boyd Paul to draw up that second set of divorce papers.

"Boyd Paul," Morgan said, "I'm sorry, but we can't do this right now."

Boyd Paul glanced at her. "Why not?"

Justin's gaze locked with hers. Ordinarily, she could tell his thoughts just by looking into his eyes, but not this time. His gaze was hooded, his expression unreadable.

Her throat felt parched. She swallowed hard.

"We have a press conference in less than a hour," she said. "They're expecting a statement from us, and we haven't even prepared one yet."

Then she briefly explained about Adam and the forged manuscript.

"We could reschedule this until tomorrow, don't you think?" she concluded. "Or maybe sometime over the weekend, when we have more time."

Or, better yet, maybe they could postpone it forever.

"Well, now, I suppose we could," Boyd Paul said, pulling a sheaf of legal papers out of his briefcase. "But I don't see why. Like I've told you, honey, this is just a formality. Shouldn't take more than ten minutes at the most. And I've got an appointment with a judge in L.A. tomorrow morning at ten. If you two can sign the papers now, we can get the final decree issued at the same time."

She shook her head. "But . . ."

Boyd Paul handed the papers to Justin.

"I'll need you to sign on the lines with the blue *X*, Professor Stone. Morgan will sign on the ones with the red." Boyd Paul grinned. "What could be simpler?"

Justin started to read the divorce agreement.

Morgan felt hot tears well up in her eyes and glanced away. Oh, what was the use of trying to stop things? she thought. She couldn't stop the divorce from happening. The most she could do was postpone it. Justin didn't want a reconciliation. He'd told her that dozens of times. Why didn't she accept the truth and let him go?

She wiped her eyes with the back of her hand. But she couldn't accept the truth.

Just as she couldn't let him go.

Heaven help her, but she loved him too damn much.

A few moments of tense silence passed.

"I can't sign this," Justin said quietly.

Her heart simply stopped. She turned toward him.

"What did you say?" she asked.

Boyd Paul frowned. "The agreement simply reiterates the conditions of the one you made in Costa Rica, Professor Stone. With a few modifications, of course. Personal assets acquired before

the marriage or after your trip to Costa Rica re-
main the property of the individual. Marital assets, such as they were, have already been taken
care of. I think it's a fair settlement, since you've
been apart for six years."

"It's not about the terms," Justin said, tossing
the papers onto the desk.

Boyd Paul scratched his head again.

"Then it must be because of that Smiley fellow," he said. "Okay. Fine. You're a little shook
up. You need more time. I can understand that.
Why don't I leave the papers with you? You can
review them after your press conference and—"

"It's not about that either," Justin interrupted. "I just don't want to sign the papers. Period."

Morgan took a step toward him.

"What are you saying, darling?" she asked,
almost afraid to breathe.

Justin met her gaze. Seconds passed.

"I'm saying that I don't want a divorce," he
said finally. "Not now. Not ever."

No one said anything for a moment. Justin
kept his gaze locked on Morgan's face. He
wanted to pull her into his arms, wanted to kiss
her until the pain he'd seen haunting her sky-blue
eyes was gone for good.

More than that, he wanted to stroke her from
her head to her toes, wanted to make love to her

until neither one of them could move a muscle, until every lingering doubt they may have still had was vanquished forever.

"I love you, Morgan," he said hoarsely, and took a step toward her. "I don't want to lose you a second time."

"Why don't I leave you two alone?" Boyd Paul murmured.

Boyd Paul snapped the lid of his briefcase closed and walked back into the outer office, carefully closing the door behind him.

"But I thought you didn't want to rush into anything," Morgan said.

Justin smiled. "I think it's a little too late to worry about that, don't you? Besides, I've thought this through. Hell, it's almost all I've thought about for the past few days."

He was quiet for a moment. "Boyd Paul did send you a letter. Mr. Dukakis signed for it Tuesday afternoon. That's the real reason he came by last night."

She stared at him. "But you told me it was to discuss routine maintenance."

"I know. I wanted to give myself a little more time with you." He moved closer still. "Are you mad at me?"

"I'm not sure."

Her eyes began to sparkle and dance with their old familiar magic. She grinned.

"Tampering with the mail's a federal offense, darling. So what did you do with the letter?"

Justin grinned back at her. "I hid it in the bookcase."

"The bookcase? Why there?"

He shrugged. "It was the first place I came to. I was desperate, Morgan. I knew what that envelope meant."

He hadn't felt ready to make the decision of whether he could trust himself enough to love her again or whether he should walk away from her the way he'd done in Costa Rica.

Now he did feel ready.

In fact, Justin had never felt more certain of anything in his entire life than he was of loving Morgan, of wanting to spend the rest of his life with her.

She ran her fingertips up his chest. Her touch burned through the fabric of his shirt to scorch his skin, brand his soul.

Her smile clouded. "I'm sorry, darling," she said softly. "I was wrong to force you into making this decision so quickly. I was wrong to think that I could pop back into your life after being away for six years and pick up things where we had left them off, wrong to think that we could—"

"Right to think we could," he corrected her. "We've changed, just as you've pointed out so many times. We've both grown up, gotten our priorities rearranged. The only thing that hasn't changed from six years ago is how much I love you . . . and how much you love me."

She flushed. "But I thought you wanted to

take things slowly," she said. "See how we fit into each other's lives before making a commitment."

"Why bother?" he asked. "I know how you fit into mine. Like poetry and fine wine, like moonlit nights and bare skin, like—"

"Chocolate and peanut butter?" She grinned again.

He laughed. "Precisely." He cupped her face in his hands. "Don't you see? Without you, I'm incomplete. I'm chocolate without the peanut butter."

He stroked her cheek, gently rubbing his thumbs across her silky skin.

"Without you I'm just sleepwalking my way through life," he said. "I might never have realized it, though, until I saw you sitting on my desk that day in my office. I honestly thought I was over you."

He shook his head in amazement.

"I honestly thought I could be satisfied with academic success. That if I threw myself into my work, my teaching, I could be happy without you. But I wasn't happy, Morgan. Not by a long shot."

He leaned down to kiss her, but she pulled away and started pacing around the room. She walked from the bookcase on one side of the office to the window on the other, back and forth, just as he'd done that first day when she'd told him they were still married.

"Darling, this is how we got into so much trouble the last time," she reminded him. "You were saying the same wonderful things to me then, about how our love was fated and kismet and all. It's hard for a girl to keep a clear head when you talk that way."

"But it's true," he said. " 'And I knew I'd love her forever, knew it even before I knew her name.' That's how it was between us. I knew I'd love you forever the moment I saw you standing in your father's kitchen. I felt the connection deep inside my soul. I knew that you were the only woman in the world for me. I love you, Morgan. Say you love me too."

"Oh, I do," she said, waving her hand at him. "Darling, you know I love you. But I want us to think this through before rushing into anything again."

She paused a moment near the window and glanced back at him. "I really don't think I could bear having to lose you a second time."

A chill shuddered through him. Nor could he bear to lose her again.

She resumed her pacing. "Maybe we could start with weekend get-togethers," she said. "I could fly out here every other week or so. And you could fly back to New Orleans occasionally. That might work. It would be sort of a trial run to see how compatible we still are."

He smiled. He knew what she was trying to do. She was offering him the compromise he'd once thought he'd wanted, offering it to him even though he knew it was far from what she wanted herself.

It made him love her all the more.

"But we're very compatible," he told her.

He reached out and took her arm. She came to a stop and met his gaze.

"Besides, weekends aren't enough," he said, pulling her closer. "Not nearly enough."

"Okay," she murmured softly.

Her husky voice sent fire-laced tremors rocketing down his spine. He drew a sharp intake of breath.

"Then maybe I could move to Santa Barbara," she said. "Find a place near the campus. I could work at the center."

"Tricia will be pleased to hear it. She told me she'd give anything to make you a permanent addition to her staff."

He eased his hands around her waist, feeling the coolness of the soft leather glide beneath his warm palms.

She flushed. "We could see each other every night, but still have our own separate residences."

"Like living together with none of the attendant responsibilities?"

"Exactly."

"Unh-unh. I want the responsibilities, Morgan. And I want you more than just for alternating weekends or for a night here and there. I want to wake up with you in my arms in the mornings and I want to go to sleep holding your body next to mine at night. I want to grow old with you and chase you down the hallways at the local rest home."

"Causing scandals left and right?" she asked breathlessly.

"And chasing you in my walker," he agreed. "I want to make love to you in the sunroom and give the staff fits. I want to inspire future generations and all that wonderful stuff we talked about."

She gently stroked his face. Her eyes glowed with love, tenderness. He'd never felt so complete, so whole.

"But what about our being from different worlds?" she asked. "And having different goals in life? Do you still believe that's true?"

He sighed. "I already told you that I was an idiot to think that way, Morgan. We have differences, but they complement each other more than they conflict. And we love each other, which is all that truly matters anyway. We can find a way to make the marriage work this time. I know we can."

He pulled her closer. His lips settled around hers. His tongue slid into her mouth, glided past her teeth to meet the gentle thrust of her own tongue. She softly moaned and wound her arms around him.

Sometime later, he reluctantly pulled away.

"Marry me, Morgan," he said huskily.

"But, darling, we're already married," she reminded him. "Costa Rica. The little paperwork snafu. Remember?"

"Then marry me again."

She grinned and straightened his tie.

"Oh, I think that can be arranged," she murmured. "But I want a church wedding this time, darling. And a wedding gown. Something with a mile and a half of French lace ought to do the trick. Cappy can give me away. He'd like that."

Justin nuzzled the side of her neck, brushing his lips against her pulse points. Each kiss made his heart thud harder, his body grow tighter.

"And Mama and Aunt Libby would want to be here too," she went on. "They're still a little annoyed about the first time, how we eloped to New Orleans and all. You know, weddings are a big deal in the South. Almost an institution."

"Fine," he murmured hoarsely. "Make the wedding as big as you want. Invite the entire state of Mississippi. I don't care. I'll go along with whatever you choose, just as long as you can put it together by this weekend."

"But, darling . . ."

"I don't want to wait a second longer than necessary to make you mine."

Her gaze met his, held it for a long while.

"But I'm already yours," she said, her voice thick with emotion. "I always have been."

He slid his lips over hers again for another kiss. And he knew it was true.

THE EDITOR'S CORNER

Along with May flowers come four terrific new LOVESWEPTs that will dazzle you with humor, excitement, and passion. Reading the best romances from the finest authors—what better way to enjoy the beauty and magic of spring?

Starting things off is the fabulous Mary Kay McComas with a love story that is the **TALK OF THE TOWN**, LOVESWEPT #738. Rosemary Wickum always finds some wonderful treasures in the refuse center, pieces perfect for her metal sculptures, but one thing she never goes looking for is a man! When recycling whiz Gary Albright begins pursuing her with shameless persistence, everyone in town starts rooting for romance. Once he nurses the embers of her passion back to life, he must convince his lady he'll always warm her heart. Irresistible characters and frisky humor make this latest Mary Kay story a tenderhearted treat—and proves that love can find us in the most unlikely places.

From the delightful Elaine Lakso comes another winner with **TASTING TROUBLE**, LOVE-SWEPT #739. Joshua Farrington doesn't think much of the Lakeview Restaurant's food or ambience, but its owner Liss Harding whets his interest and provokes him into a brash charade! Tempting her with strawberries, kissing her in the wine cellar, Josh coaxes her to renovate the building, update the menu —and lose herself in his arms. But once he confesses his identity, he has to persuade her he isn't the enemy. As delectable as chocolate, as intoxicating as fine wine, this wonderful romance from Elaine introduces charming, complex lovers whose dreams are more alike than they can imagine.

From the ever-popular Erica Spindler comes **SLOW HEAT**, LOVESWEPT #740. Jack Jacobs thrives on excitement, thrills to a challenge, and always plays to win, so when the sexy TV film critic is teamed with Jill Lansing, he expects fireworks! Five years before, they'd been wildly, recklessly in love, but he couldn't give her the promise she'd craved. Now she needs a hero, a man who'll share his soul at last. He is her destiny, her perfect partner in work and in bed, but can Jill make him understand he has to fight for what he wants—and that her love is worth fighting for? Steamy with innuendo, sparkling with wit, Erica's exhilarating battle of the sexes reunites a fiery pair of lovers—and casts an enchanting spell!

Rising star Maris Soule offers a hero who is full of **DARK TEMPTATION**, LOVESWEPT #741. Did special-effects genius Jason McLain really murder his wife, as the tabloids claimed? Valerie Wiggins approaches his spooky old house, hoping to convince him to help her make their Halloween charity event truly frightening. But when he opens the door, her heart races not with fright but sizzling arousal. Jason fears caring for Val will put her in danger, but maybe helping her face her demons will silence his own. Torn by doubts, burning with desire, can a man and a woman who'd first touched in darkness find themselves healed by the dawn? In a heartstopping novel of passion and suspense, Maris explores our deepest terrors and most poignant longings in the journey that transforms strangers into soulmates.

Happy reading!

With warmest wishes,

Beth de Guzman   Shauna Summers
Senior Editor   Associate Editor

P.S. Don't miss the women's novels coming your way in May: **DARK RIDER** from *The New York Times* bestselling author Iris Johansen is an electrifying tale of deadly and forbidden desire that sweeps from the exotic islands of a tropical paradise to the magnificent estates of Regency England; **LOVE STORM** by Susan Johnson, the bestselling mistress of the erotic historical romance, is the legendary, long out-of-print novel of tempestuous passion; **PROMISE ME MAGIC** by the extraordinary Patricia Camden is a "Once Upon a Time" historical romance of passion and adventure in the tradition of Laura Kinsale. And immediately following this page, look for a preview of the exciting romances from Bantam that are *available now!*

Don't miss these extraordinary books
by your favorite Bantam authors

On sale in March:

MISTRESS
by Amanda Quick

DANGEROUS TO KISS
by Elizabeth Thornton

LONG NIGHT MOON
by Theresa Weir

MISTRESS

Available in paperback
by the *New York Times*
bestselling author

AMANDA QUICK

DANGEROUS TO KISS
by Elizabeth Thornton

"A major, major talent . . . a genre superstar."
—*Rave Reviews*

Handsome, kind, and unassuming, Mr. Gray seemed the answer to Deborah Weyman's prayers. For once she accepted the position he offered, she would finally be safe from the notorious Lord Kendal, a man she had good reason to believe had murdered her former employer—and was now after her. But there were certain things about Mr. Gray that Deborah should have noticed: the breadth of his shoulders, the steel in his voice, the gleam in his uncommonly blue eyes—things that might have warned her that Mr. Gray was no savior but a very dangerous man. . . .

"Study hall," said Deborah brightly, addressing Mr. Gray, and all the girls groaned.

With a few muttered protests and a great deal of snickering, the girls began to file out of the room. Deborah assisted their progress by holding the door for them, reminding them cheerfully that on the morrow they would be reviewing irregular French verbs and she expected them to have mastered their conjugations. As the last girl slipped by her, Deborah shut the door with a snap, then rested her back against it, taking a moment or two to collect herself.

Suddenly aware that Mr. Gray had risen at their exit and was standing awkwardly by the window, she politely invited him to be seated. "You'll have a glass of sherry?" she inquired. At Miss Hare's, the guests were invariably treated to a glass of sherry when the ordeal of taking tea was over. At his nod, Deborah moved to the sideboard against the wall. The glasses and decanter were concealed behind a locked door, and she had to stoop to retrieve them from their hiding place.

As he seated himself, Gray's gaze wandered over the lush curves of her bottom. There was an appreciative glint in his eye. The thought that was going through his head was that Deborah Weyman bore no resemblance to the descriptions he had been given of her. Spinsterish? Straitlaced? Dull and uninteresting? That's what she wanted people to think. She had certainly dressed for the part with her high-necked, long-sleeved blue kerseymere and the unbiquitous white mobcap pulled down to cover her hair. An untrained eye would look no further. Unhappily for the lady, not only was he a trained observer, but he was also an acknowledged connoisseur of women. Advantage to him.

Since her attention was riveted on the two glasses of sherry on the tray she was carrying, he took the liberty of studying her at leisure. Her complexion was tinged with gray—powder, he presumed—in an attempt to add years and dignity to sculpted bones that accredited beauties of the *ton* would kill for. The shapeless gown served her no better than the gray face powder. She had the kind of figure that would look good in the current high-waisted diaphanous gauzes or in sackcloth and ashes. Soft, curvaceous, womanly. When she handed him his sherry, he kept his expression blank. Behind the wire-rimmed spectacles, her lustrous green eyes were framed by— he blinked and looked again. Damned if she had not snipped at her eyelashes to shorten them! Had the woman no vanity?

"I missed something, didn't I?" said Deborah. "That's why you are smiling that secret smile to yourself."

"Beg pardon?" Gray's thick veil of lashes lowered to diffuse the intentness of her look.

Deborah seated herself. "I missed something when Millicent offered you a cucumber sandwich. What was it?"

If he had the dressing of her, the first thing he would do was banish the mobcap. There wasn't a curl or stray tendril of hair to be seen. "A note."

"A note?"

"Mmm." Red hair or blond. It had to be one or the other. Unless she had dyed it, of course. He wouldn't put it past her. If this were a tavern and she were not a lady, he would offer her fifty, no, a hundred gold guineas if only she would remove that blasted cap.

"Are you saying that Millicent passed you a note?"

Her voice had returned to its prim and proper mode. He was beginning to understand why she had kept out of the public eye. She couldn't sustain a part.

"The note," Deborah reminded him gently.

"The note? Ah, yes, the note. It was in the cucumber sandwich." She was trying to suppress a smile, and her dimples fascinated him. No one had mentioned that she had dimples.

"Oh dear, I suppose I should show it to Miss Hare. That girl is incorrigible."

"I'm afraid that won't be possible."

"Why won't it?"

"On her way out, she snatched it back. I believe she ate it."

When she laughed, he relaxed against the back of his chair, well pleased with himself. That wary, watchful look that had hovered at the back of her eyes had completely dissipated. He was beginning to take her measure. The more he erased his masculinity, the more trustful she became. Unhappily for him, there was something about Deborah Weyman that stirred the softer side of his nature. Advantage to her.

Deborah sipped at her sherry, trying to contain her impatience. As her prospective employer, it was up to him to begin the interview. He lacked the social graces. She wasn't finding fault with him. On the contrary, his inexperience appealed to her. It made him seem awkward, boyish, harmless. Besides, she had enough social graces for the two of them.

"Miss Hare mentioned that you were seeking a governess for your young sister?" she said.

He was reluctant to get down to business. All too soon, things would change. That trustful look would be gone from her eyes, and Miss Weyman would never trust him again. Pity, but that was almost inevitable. Still, he wasn't going to make things difficult for her at this stage of the game. That would come later.

Deborah shifted restlessly. "You will wish to know

about references from former employers," she said, trying to lead him gently.

"References?" He relaxed a little more comfortably against the back of his chair. Smiling crookedly, he said, "Oh, Miss Hare explained your circumstances to me. Having resided in Ireland with your late husband for a goodly number of years, you allowed your acquaintance with former employers to lapse."

"That is correct."

"I quite understand. Besides, Miss Hare's recommendation carries more weight with me."

"Thank you." She'd got over the first hurdle. Really, it was as easy as taking sweetmeats from a babe. Mr. Gray was more gullible than she could have hoped. The thought shamed her, and her eyes slid away from his.

"Forgive me for asking," he said, "Miss Hare did not make this clear to me. She mentioned that in addition to teaching my sister the correct forms and addresses, you would also impart a little gloss. How do you propose to do that?"

There was an awkward pause, then Mr. Gray brought his glass to his lips and Deborah shrank involuntarily. She knew that she looked like the last person on earth who could impart gloss to anyone.

For a long, introspective moment, she stared at her clasped hands. Seeing that look, Gray asked quietly, "What is it? What have I said?" and leaning over, he drew one finger lightly across her wrist.

The touch of his finger on her bare skin sent a shock of awareness to all the pulse points in her body. She trembled, stammered, then fell silent. When she raised her eyes to his, she had herself well in hand. "I know what you are thinking," she said.

"Do you? I doubt it." He, too, had felt the shock of awareness as bare skin slid over bare skin. The pull on his senses astonished him.

His eyes were as soft as his smile. Disregarding both, she said earnestly, "You must understand, Mr. Gray, that governesses and schoolteachers are not paid to be fashionable. Indeed, employers have a decided preference for governesses who know their place. Servants wear livery. We governesses wear a livery of sorts, too. Well, you must have noticed that the schoolteachers at Miss Hare's are almost indistinguishable, one from the other."

"You are mistaken. I would know you anywhere."

LONG NIGHT MOON

by the spectacular

Theresa Weir

"Theresa Weir's writing is poignant, passionate and powerful . . . will capture the hearts of readers."
—*New York Times* bestselling author Jayne Ann Krentz

With her rare insight into the human heart, Theresa Weir creates tender, emotionally compelling, powerfully satisfying love stories. Now the author whom Romantic Times *praises as "a fresh and electrifying voice in romantic fiction," offers* LONG NIGHT MOON, *a novel that touches on the nationally important issue of domestic violence and affirms the power of love to heal the deepest sorrows.*

"I don't know what the hell—" His voice caught.

She was lying on her side, facing the window, clasped hands under her head, knees drawn up, eyes open wide, staring at nothing. And she was crying. Without making a sound.

Oh, Christ.

He was a man with no heart, no conscience, but suddenly he ached with an ache that was unbearable.

An ache that tightened his throat and stung his eyes. An ache he remembered but had never wanted to experience again.

For once in his life, he was at a total loss. He didn't speak. He didn't know what to say.

She pulled in a trembling breath. The sound seemed to fill the quiet of the room, adding weight to the ache in his chest. And then she spoke. Quietly, emotionlessly, her very lack of feeling a reflection of her measured control, of words doled out with utmost care.

"I thought I could be somebody else. At least for a little while."

He had no idea what to do, but he found himself pulling her into his arms. He held her, and he rocked her. He breathed in the scent of her. He stroked her hair, letting the satin tresses slide through his fingers.

Instinctively he knew that this was the real Sara Ivy. Not the socialite with her expensive gowns and jewels, not the hard woman who had snubbed him.

And the woman on the beach—she, too, was Sara Ivy. Defiant. Brave. Sexy.

That one drove him crazy.

But this one . . . this one broke his heart.

Time passed. The clock on the desk made its old familiar grinding sound.

Nine o'clock.

Sara lifted her head from his shoulder and let out a sigh. "I have to go."

Feeling strangely fragile, he let her slip out of his arms. Her body left a warm, invisible imprint on him.

She stood, gripping the blanket under her chin. "Don't watch me dress."

He had seen her naked body. He had a photo he stared at almost daily, a photo he'd lied to her about.

He turned. He walked toward the windows. With one finger, he pushed at the blinds. Metal popped, bent, making a triangle he could look through.

The full December moon. Low in the sky, blurry, as if a storm was moving in.

"Don't go," he said quietly, without turning around.

"I have to."

"Why?" He didn't want to think about her going back to Ivy.

She didn't say anything.

He made it a point to avoid intimate conversations, but suddenly he wanted her to talk to him, wanted her to explain things.

Rather than suffer the intrusive glare of a sixty-watt bulb, he opened the blinds, letting in just the right amount of light.

Behind him, he heard her move, heard the soft whisper of her shoes as she crossed the room.

He turned.

She was dressed and slipping into her coat. Her clothes seemed to have given her strength. Some of that cool, aloof control was back.

She went to the phone and called for a cab.

Anger— or was it fear—leaped in him. "What happens if you get home late?" he asked, his voice bordering on sarcasm. "Does he cut off your allowance?"

She silently considered him.

For the last several years, he'd prided himself on

the fact that he knew more about life than anybody. It was an arrogant assumption. Suddenly that truth was never more apparent. As she stared at him, the foundation of his self-assurance wobbled, and he experience a moment of doubt.

He had a sudden image of himself, standing next to a yawning precipice, ready to tumble headlong.

"Yes," she said with a smile that hinted at self-mockery.

He remembered that this was the woman who had tried to kill herself.

"He takes away my allowance."

They were talking around the problem, talking around what had just happened, or hadn't happened, between them.

"I don't get it," he said, frustration getting the best of him. He wanted solid answers. "Why did you come here? To spite him?" Then he had another thought, a thought that fit more with his original opinion of Sara Ivy. "Or was it to get yourself dirty, only to find you couldn't go through with it?"

She looked away, some of her newly regained composure slipping. "I . . . I, ah . . ." She swallowed. She pressed her lips together. "I was willing to make a trade," she said so softly he hardly heard her. "At least I thought I was." She shrugged her shoulders and let out a nervous little laugh. "Sex just doesn't seem to be a good means of barter for me." She clasped her hands together. "Perhaps if you'd wanted something else, anything else, it might have worked."

"What are you talking about?"

"Sex. That was your ultimatum, wasn't it?"

The room seemed to slant.

What had happened to him? How had he gotten so heartless?

There had been a time when he'd been more naive than Harley. There had been a time when he'd been a nice guy, too. And he'd been hurt. And he'd decided to get tough or be eaten alive. But this . . . Oh, God.

"I have to go."

Her words came to him through a thick haze.

"W-wait." Shaking, he grabbed a sweatshirt, then managed to stuff his feet into a pair of sneakers. "I'll walk you."

They made their way down the stairs, then down the hallway.

Outside, the moon was completely obliterated by snowflakes drifting earthward. They were huge—like tissue-paper cutouts, floating on the still air.

Sara's face was lifted to the night sky. "Snow." Her voice held the wonder of a child.

He watched as wet flakes kissed her cheeks, her hair, her eyelashes, melting against her skin. When she looked back at him, she was smiling. Not the self-mocking smile he'd seen earlier, but a soft, slow, real smile.

The wall he'd put up, the barrier he'd worked so hard and so diligently to build, crumbled.

And he knew, in that second, from that point on, that nothing would be the same.

He would never be able to look at the world with the same detachment, the same distance, the same lack of emotion.

They hadn't made love. Their bodies hadn't

joined, but *something* had happened. She had somehow, some way, touched his soul.

He, who had sworn never to love anyone again, watched her with a feeling of helplessness. He watched as snowflakes continued to fall on her face and hair and eyelashes.

A benediction.

He took one faltering step, then another.

Ever since the night on the beach, he'd known that he had to have her, possess her. But now everything had suddenly turned around.

Now he wanted more.

He stopped directly in front of her. Slowly, her face was drawn to his. Her smile faded. A question came into her eyes.

Slowly, carefully, he took her face in his hands, cupping her cold cheeks against his warm palms, watching as their breaths mingled. He lowered his head, watching as her eyes fluttered closed, as her face lifted to his.

His own eyes closed. And then there was just the softness of her lips.

Her hair slid over his wrist. Her hands came up around his neck.

He pulled her closer, bulky coat and all, his mouth moving over hers. Her lips parted, inviting his tongue. And when he slid it against hers, his heart pounded, his body throbbed.

A horn honked.

Reality.

A hand to her chin, he broke the kiss. Her eyelashes fluttered. She looked dazed, slightly disoriented.

"I'm sorry about what I said the night of Harley's party." His voice came out tight and strained and a little lost. "I sometimes say things I don't mean, just because . . . well, because I'm an ass." He brushed a finger across her bottom lip. "Come and see me anytime. We can play Monopoly. Or watch TV. Do you like to look at stars? I have lawn chairs set up on the roof of Shoot the Moon."

Honk.

She blinked, glanced over her shoulder, then back. "I have to go."

He wanted to extract a promise from her. He wanted her to tell him that she'd be back, that he would see her again. He loosened his hold and she slipped away.

She ran to the cab.

He followed, closing the door for her once she was inside. As the cab pulled away, he could see her watching him through the glass.

She lifted her hand in farewell.

Pathos. A word Harley had dug out of him, its meaning just now truly hitting home.

He lifted his own hand, the slow, lingering gesture mirroring hers.

How could one simple movement hurt so much? How could it be so bittersweet?

And don't miss these electrifying romances from Bantam Books, on sale in April:

DARK RIDER
by the *New York Times* bestselling author
Iris Johansen
"Iris Johansen is one of the romance genre's finest treasures."
—*Romantic Times*

MASTER OF PARADISE
by the highly acclaimed
Katherine O'Neal
"Katherine O'Neal is the queen of romantic adventure."
—*Affaire de Coeur*

PROMISE ME MAGIC
by the spectacular
Patricia Camden
"A strong new voice in historical fiction . . . an author to watch!"
—*Romantic Times*